“Men think with their heads. Not their hearts,” she murmured more to herself than to him.

“Not always.”

That brought her head around and as she studied his profile illuminated by the dash panel lights, she wondered if he’d ever trusted his heart to a woman and had it broken. She couldn’t imagine him grieving over a broken romance. She could, however, imagine him having passionate sex without promises or strings attached.

“Are you married, Dr. Hollister?”

His short laugh was an answer in itself. “No. I barely have time to eat, much less see after a wife and kids.”

For some inexplicable reason, his response saddened her. “Well, it’s good that you know your limitations.”

“Hmm. I didn’t know I had limitations. I just thought I was a busy man.”

She forced herself to smile. “Sorry. You’ll have to overlook me. I’m rather tired and things aren’t coming out of my mouth exactly right.”

“Well, just a few more miles and we’ll be at Three Rivers.”

Three Rivers. Each time he said the name, it was like he was speaking of a place close to heaven. And for this one night, that was exactly what she needed.

MEN OF THE WEST:

Whether ranchers or lawmen, these heartbreakers can ride, shoot—and drive a woman crazy...

Dear Reader,

Spring comes early to Yavapai County, Arizona, and now that May has arrived, the calves have been born and the new foals are already standing strong at their mothers' sides. But that hardly means the work lets up on Three Rivers Ranch. Especially for veterinarian Chandler Hollister. His animal hospital is always overflowing with needy patients—the four-legged kind, that is. A pregnant woman suffering a fainting spell isn't normally included in his daily schedule.

When Roslyn DuBose stops her car on the outskirts of Wickenburg, she's only seeking a few minutes of rest. Her long journey won't end until she reaches California, where she can hopefully put her mistakes in the past. Her plans definitely don't include a sexy cowboy with a stethoscope around his neck!

But Chandler takes one look at the pregnant runaway and decides she needs to take a detour to Three Rivers Ranch, and straight into his arms!

I hope you enjoy reading how this special Hollister man comes to realize he needs a family of his own and how Roslyn learns that a home is anywhere the heart is content.

God bless the trails you ride,

Stella Bagwell

His Texas Runaway

Stella Bagwell

Recycling programs for this product may not exist in your area.

ISBN-13: 978-1-335-57384-1

His Texas Runaway

This edition published by arrangement with Harlequin Books S.A.

For questions and comments about the quality of this book, please contact us at CustomerService@Harlequin.com.

Printed in U.S.A.

After writing more than eighty books for Harlequin, **Stella Bagwell** still finds it exciting to create new stories and bring her characters to life. She loves all things Western and has been married to her own real cowboy for forty-four years. Living on the south Texas coast, she also enjoys being outdoors and helping her husband care for the horses, cats and dog that call their small ranch home. The couple has one son, who teaches high school mathematics and is also an athletic director. Stella loves hearing from readers. They can contact her at stellabagwell@gmail.com.

Books by Stella Bagwell

Harlequin Special Edition

Men of the West

The Arizona Lawman
Her Man on Three Rivers Ranch
A Ranger for Christmas

The Fortunes of Texas: The Lost Fortunes

Guarding His Fortune

Montana Mavericks: The Lonelyhearts Ranch

The Little Maverick Matchmaker

Montana Mavericks: The Great Family Roundup

The Maverick's Bride-to-Order

The Fortunes of Texas: The Secret Fortunes

Her Sweetest Fortune

Visit the Author Profile page
at Harlequin.com for more titles.

To my beloved paint horse, Little Giant Sequoia,
who paced the fence until his daughter
was safely born.

Chapter One

Roslyn DuBose switched on the headlights and peered at the navigation map illuminated on the dashboard of her car. Wickenburg, Arizona, was less than three miles away. Surely she could hang on until she reached the small desert town. Pulling off to the side of a dark, lonely highway, even for a short rest, wasn't a safe option. Not for her, or her unborn baby.

Gripping the steering wheel, she blinked and hoped the cobwebs in front of her weary eyes would go away. For the past two days she'd driven over a thousand miles and fatigue was beginning to overtake her. Tonight she had no choice but to settle in for a rest. Hopefully when her father read the note she'd left for him back in Fort Worth, he'd understand and not intervene. But Martin DuBose wasn't an understanding or forgiving man. Sooner or later, he'd come after her.

Determined, Roslyn drove onward, toward the lights

dotting the dark horizon. Until the two-lane highway seemed to be coming at her in undulating waves.

God help her, she was going to faint!

The horrifying thought was zipping through her brain at the same time she spotted a brick building with a wide graveled parking area.

Wheeling the car to a halt beneath the dim glow of a security light, she turned off the engine and reached for a water bottle resting in the cup holder next to her seat.

Damn. It was empty. When had she downed the last of the water? Winslow? Flagstaff?

Resting her head against the seat, she splayed a hand upon the large mound where her waist used to be and felt the child moving against the bottom of her rib cage.

Hang on, little darlin'. In a minute I'll feel better. Then I'll find us a nice meal and a soft bed.

Another kick landed somewhere in the region of her bellybutton and if Roslyn hadn't been so exhausted she would've smiled at the notion of the baby reading her thoughts. For now, she was barely able to muster enough energy to peer beyond the windshield at the sign hanging over the door of the building.

Hollister Animal Clinic.

She'd parked in front of a veterinary clinic that appeared to be closed for the night. At least no one was around to accuse her of loitering, she thought, as she leaned her forehead against the steering wheel.

Just a minute or two more of rest, she promised herself, and then she'd move on.

On a normal day, Chandler Hollister tried to close his veterinarian business at six in the evening. But his days were rarely normal. On most evenings, he went far past seven or even eight at night, performing last-minute surgeries or dealing with emergencies that couldn't wait until morning. Such was the case tonight.

The last three hours he'd spent driving to a ranch in a remote corner of Yavapai County, then riding horseback to a rugged arroyo to doctor one cow who'd had difficulty calving. Being the only vet in the area made his job challenging, but he wouldn't change it for anything.

Now, as he drove the last half mile to Hollister Animal Clinic, he glanced at the digital clock on the truck dashboard. "Eight fifteen. Not too bad considering I've been up since four thirty this morning. I might actually get home to Three Rivers before ten tonight."

In the seat across from him, Chandler's young assistant let out a weary groan. "You might be feeling like a stud colt, but I'm dead beat. And we still have the horses to unload and put to bed for the night."

Chuckling, Chandler nudged the brim of his gray Stetson back off his forehead. "Trey, you're thirty years old. Six years younger than me. You should have energy to spare."

Trey grunted. "I'm not used to working sixteen hours a day, six days a week, like you are."

"You should be getting used to it," Chandler said wryly. "You've done it for the past two years."

"Yeah, and what am I getting for it? Besides a paycheck and a continual state of exhaustion?"

Chandler grinned. "Fulfillment, Trey. You can go home tonight knowing that cow and her little baby are going to be fine."

"They won't be fine if she and the baby can't climb out of the arroyo. If it rains—"

Chandler's laugh interrupted his words. "Rain? Are you kidding? There's no danger of seeing a drop of it for weeks. Besides, if it did start raining, old Amos would winch the pair out to higher ground."

"You're right. That old man is just like you, he'd try to help a sidewinder if he thought it was sick."

"Sometimes snakes need doctoring, too," Chandler replied.

The familiar sight of the clinic came into view and Trey promptly scooted to the edge of his seat. "Hey, Doc, a car is parked in front of the building. Sure doesn't look like it belongs to any of the girls, either."

Chandler flipped on the turn signal and steered the truck into the clinic's parking area. As he peered at the light-colored car parked at an angle to the building, he decided Trey's assessment was right. There wasn't a chance the unfamiliar vehicle belonged to any one of his staff.

"No," Chandler agreed. "That's a Jaguar. A fairly new one, at that."

Trey whistled under his breath. "Must be Mrs. Whitley with one of her Siamese cats. She's wealthy enough to drive a Jag. But how would the woman know you'd be back here tonight?"

"I doubt Mrs. Whitley would splurge on a luxury car. She's as miserly as her late husband used to be. But she'd win the trophy for showing up after hours." He drove on past the building and parked the truck and trailer near a maze of sheds and holding pens. "Take the horses on to the barn. I'll check out the car."

Trey opened the door and jumped to the ground. "Guess you're going to open up and take care of that damn cat."

"If need be. Or if you'd rather, I'll take care of the horses and you can deal with the cat," Chandler offered with a baiting grin.

"Oh, hell no. I've had enough scratches and bites for this month."

"Trey, it's only the second day of April."

"That's my point, Doc."

Chuckling, Chandler left Trey to deal with the horses and walked down a short slope to where the car was parked near the entrance of the clinic. The lights were off, and the tinted windows were up, making it difficult to see whether anyone was inside.

He rapped his knuckles on the driver's door and called out, "Hey, anyone in there?"

Long seconds passed without any response and Chandler was about to decide the car was empty when the window slid down a few inches and he found himself peering into a woman's wide, wary eyes.

"The clinic is closed for the night," Chandler told her. "Do you have an emergency?"

"Emergency?"

"An emergency with an animal," Chandler patiently explained. "Do you have a pet with you in the car?"

The eyes that had been warily studying him blinked and then the window lowered to reveal a very young woman. "Uh…no. No animal. I, uh, just stopped for a minute—to rest."

Frowning, he stepped closer. "Excuse me, miss, but you don't sound well. Do you need to get out and—"

Finishing the question would've been pointless as she suddenly flopped face-forward onto the steering wheel.

Recognizing she'd fainted, Chandler jerked on the door handle, only to discover it was locked. Without hesitation, he reached through the open window and released the latch.

Once the door swung wide, he leaned in and touched her shoulder. When she failed to respond, he felt for a pulse at the base of her neck. The faint, rapid thump wasn't ideal, but at least her heart was beating.

Carefully, he eased her head away from the wheel and touched a hand to her face. Beneath his palm, the soft skin felt clammy.

He was trying to decide whether to call an ambulance or carry her into the clinic, when she suddenly began to rouse.

"Ooh." She groaned and looked up at him. "Where... am I?"

"You're in Wickenburg. You're in your car," he calmly informed her. "Have you been ill?"

While Chandler waited for her to answer, his gaze dropped to the very pregnant belly touching the bottom of the steering wheel. Oh, damn. If she was a mare, he'd predict she wasn't far away from foaling.

Her brow furrowed with confusion. "No. I haven't been sick. I've been driving for a long time. If I could just trouble you for a drink of water—that's all I need."

He eased her shoulder back against the seat. "Don't try to move," he ordered. "I'll be right back."

Chandler hurriedly unlocked the heavy glass door on the front of the building and returned to the car. By then, she was sitting up straight and wiping a hand over her face.

"Let me help you into the clinic," he said. "Or if you think the baby is coming, I'll drive you to the hospital."

The hand on her face instantly fell to her belly. "Oh, I don't need a hospital. The baby isn't coming." She looked up at him. "I—I'm sorry to bother you. I got swimmy-headed and thought I'd better rest before I drove on. I can make it now."

Her face was as pale as the moon rising over the distant hill behind him. She wasn't in any shape to drive ten feet, much less a mile and a half, he decided.

He extended his hand out to her and ordered, "I'm not so sure. Take my hand and squeeze it."

She frowned. "Why?"

"Don't worry. I'm a doctor. My name is Chandler Hollister and I own this veterinary clinic where you've parked."

"Oh. You're an animal doctor."

He couldn't help grinning. "I've been known to doctor a few humans from time to time. After all, we're mostly two-legged animals."

"Uh… I suppose." She hesitated a moment, then finally placed her hand in his. "Nice to meet you, Dr. Hollister. I'm Roslyn DuBose.

Her fingers managed to fold around his, but he likened the touch to the gentle closing of a butterfly's wings. "Is that the most you can squeeze, Roslyn?"

"I'm sorry," she murmured. "I'm rather tired."

He didn't wait for her to say more. He leaned in closer and ordered, "Put your arms around my neck."

"Listen, Doctor, if this is another of your tests, I'm—"

"It's not a test. Put your arms around my neck. I'm going to carry you into the clinic."

"Oh, but I can walk," she protested. "Just give me a hand."

"You can walk later. Right now, do as I say."

To his relief, she followed his orders and he lifted her out of the car and into his arms.

As he started toward the clinic with her, Trey came jogging up to them.

"What the hell, Doc? She's not a cat!"

"Far from it," he told his assistant. "Go down to my office and make sure the couch is cleaned off. This young lady needs a few minutes of rest."

"Right. I got it."

At the entrance, the tall, lanky blond held the door open long enough for Chandler to step inside with his armload, then he sped down the hallway ahead of them.

By the time Chandler reached his private office, Trey had cleared the couch of clutter and propped a pillow at one end.

"Is she about to have the baby?" Trey asked as he stood to one side, watching anxiously as Chandler placed his latest patient on the couch. "Should I call the ambulance?"

Chandler carefully positioned the pillow beneath her head. "No. And no. Not yet, anyway," he told Trey. "Right now, I need a bottle of water from the fridge."

Trey fetched him the water, then Chandler squatted down at her side, quickly twisted off the lid and tilted the bottle to her lips.

"Drink, Ms. DuBose," he prompted. "It will help revive you."

She wrapped a hand around the bottle and drank thirstily. Once she had her fill, she said, "I'm so sorry about this. I don't want to be a bother to either of you."

"Don't worry." Chandler tried to reassure her with a gentle smile. "We're used to putting in overtime."

She leaned her head back against the pillow and drew in a long breath. "This is all my fault. I've been driving all day and haven't taken a break since I passed through Flagstaff."

"You're trying to get to your destination tonight?" Chandler's gaze roamed her face. He was an expert at gauging an animal's accurate age, especially horses. But humans were a different matter. Especially women. If he had to guess Ms. DuBose's age, the best he could narrow it down to was somewhere between twenty and twenty-five.

She had warm brown eyes that reminded him of toffee candy. Light brown hair fringed her forehead and waved gently to the tops of her shoulders. At the moment, her dusky pink lips were parted just enough to show the edges of very white teeth. Altogether, she was very lovely.

"I was only trying to reach Wickenburg tonight," she answered. "I, uh, planned to stay a couple of days here before I traveled on to… California."

She seemed hesitant about adding the last bit of information, but that was understandable, Chandler thought. He and Trey were total strangers to her.

"Good idea. You obviously need to rest." He walked over to a row of cabinets and pulled a blood-pressure cuff from a drawer, then plucked a stethoscope from the pocket of a lab coat hanging from a hall tree. "Let me see how you're ticking and then you might try to eat something."

She pointed to the blood-pressure cuff. "That's the kind you use on people. I must really be disoriented. I thought you said this was an animal clinic."

"Don't worry, miss," Trey said. "Sometimes folks that bring in their animals keel over themselves. Doc takes care of them, too."

Her expression skeptical, she said, "Oh. I guess it's my good fortune I stopped here."

"More like Trey's good fortune," Chandler said, as he once again squatted next to the couch and reached for Roslyn's arm. "He likes rescuing damsels in distress."

Trey's face reddened. "Oh, Doc, that's not so and you know it."

Chandler wrapped the cuff around her slender arm and pumped it tight. She remained quiet as he noted the numbers, but he could feel her gaze wandering over his face.

He figured he looked like hell to her and smelled

even worse. Long before daylight this morning he'd been called out on an emergency and hadn't taken time to shave. Since then he'd waded through cow and horse manure, tromped through pigpens and bloodied his jeans and shirt while castrating several colts.

From the looks of Roslyn DuBose, he figured she was accustomed to seeing men in suits and ties and wing-tips that never touched anything dirtier than a concrete sidewalk.

"Do I have a blood pressure, Dr. Hollister?" she asked with dry amusement.

Her soft voice pulled his attention back to her face. How would she look without the dark smudges of fatigue beneath her eyes and the tension at the corners of her mouth? Something or someone was definitely making her anxious.

"You do. Although it's still a little low. The water should help that. Drink all you can." He hung the stethoscope around his neck and started to rise, but at the last moment changed his mind. "Would you like for me to listen to the baby? Just to make sure he or she isn't in distress?"

"Oh, yes. I'd be very grateful.

He positioned the stethoscope back in his ears and placed the round metal diaphragm against her belly. After listening intently at several different spots, he gave her a thumbs-up sign.

"Sounds like a healthy girl. Is that what it is?"

She shook her head. "I don't know. I wanted to find out the gender the old-fashioned way. But I've been calling it a boy. Do you really think it's a girl?"

"Well, my brothers say I'm an expert at predicting a foal's gender. But that doesn't mean you should go out and buy everything in pink."

He walked back over to the cabinet to put away the

blood-pressure cuff and stethoscope. "Trey, did you see anything in the fridge to eat? The girls usually leave their lunch leftovers."

Trey said, "I think there's a piece of fried chicken and one of those cartons of yogurt. That's all."

"That's enough." He glanced over his shoulder to see the woman had relaxed enough to close her eyes. Chandler motioned for Trey to follow him out of the room.

Out in the hallway, the two men made their way to a stockroom, where medical supplies were stored on shelves and in refrigerators.

As Chandler rummaged through one of the refrigerators for the food, Trey asked in a hushed voice, "What do you think about her?"

"She's going to be okay. As far as I can tell, she's suffering from dehydration and exhaustion."

"No. I don't mean medically. I mean, what is she doing here? In Wickenburg?"

Chandler shot him a droll look. "I wouldn't know that any more than you. From what she says, she's on her way to California. Frankly, it's not our business."

Trey lifted his straw hat from his head, then plopped it back down as though the action would help him think. "Well, she sure is pretty."

"Yeah, she sure is."

"Wonder where her husband is. The guy must be an idiot for letting her get on the road in that condition."

"I'm not sure she has a husband."

Trey eyes widened. "What makes you think that, Doc? Did you ask her?"

"No. I didn't ask her. It's just an assumption. She isn't wearing a ring."

"Maybe that's because her hands are swollen and the

ring is too tight. My sister's hands stayed puffy when she was pregnant."

"Trey, you're watching too much TV. You're getting the idea you're a PI in a cowboy hat."

"Oh, shoot, I'm just trying to figure her out," Trey reasoned. "We don't ever get anyone like her here at the clinic."

Chandler placed the piece of chicken on a paper plate, then found a plastic spoon to go with the carton of yogurt. "I wouldn't start setting my sights on her, Trey. She'll be gone in a couple of days."

Trey snorted. "Hell, I'm not going to be guilty of setting my sights on any woman. I can barely take care of myself. But she's easy on the eyes. And I sorta feel bad for her. She seems kinda lost, don't you think?"

Chandler let out a long breath. In the twelve years since he'd opened the clinic, Trey was the best assistant he'd ever had. But sometimes the man's incessant chatter had Chandler longing for a piece of duct tape. However, this was one time Trey was voicing Chandler's exact thoughts.

"She'll be okay, Trey," Chandler reiterated. "And if you're finished with the horses, you can go on home. I can handle this. There's no need for you to keep hanging around."

Trey looked at him with surprise and then he grinned and winked. "I got it, Doc. You'd rather be alone with the lady. No problem. I'm out of here. Pronto. Like right now."

Chandler hardly needed to be alone with Roslyn DuBose. Not in the way Trey was suggesting. But he did need time to make sure she was capable of leaving the clinic under her own power. "I'll see you in the morning. At six. Remember? We have to be over to the Johnson ranch to geld his colts."

"Six. Yeah, I'll be here." He screwed his hat down tighter on his head and started out the door. "You can tell me all about Ms. DuBose then."

Roslyn pushed herself to a sitting position on the couch and glanced curiously around Dr. Hollister's office. The room was nothing like her OB's plush office and definitely nothing close to the luxurious suites that made up her father's corporate law firm back in Fort Worth.

Rectangular in shape, this office had a bare concrete floor and walls of whitewashed cinderblock. A large metal desk with a leather executive chair took up most of the left-hand side of the space. Two wooden chairs sat at odd angles in front of the desk that was used for consultations, she supposed. Although, the seats were presently filled with an odd assortment of clothing and leather riding tack. To the right of her, metal cabinets and shelves were loaded with boxes of medications and other medical supplies, while straight in front of her the wall was covered with an endless number of photographs, all involving animals. Most of the images were of horses, taken either in the winners' circle at the racetrack, or in an arena next to a trophy-presentation table. Along with the horses, there were pics of dogs, cats, raccoons and opossums.

The man clearly had an affinity for animals, she decided. And he had no need to surround himself with a lavish work area. The fact impressed her, almost as much as the gentleness of his hands and the kindness she'd found in his eyes.

She was still thinking about him when he suddenly walked through the door carrying a plate of food. As he moved toward her, she found her gaze riveted to his striking image.

He was at least an inch or two over six feet, and his

shoulders were so broad they stretched the denim fabric of his Western shirt to the limit. As her eyes followed the line of pearl snaps down to a square, silver belt buckle, she noted that his lean waist was a huge contrast to the breadth of his shoulders. Long, muscular legs strained against the work-worn denim.

Lifting her gaze, she studied his rugged features, which were made up of a square chin, and a jaw, covered with dark, rusty stubble. Beneath the gray cowboy hat, his hair was dark enough to call black and lay in thick waves until it reached the back of his collar. His eyes were vivid blue, like the sky after a hard rain, and framed by thick black lashes. The effect of his gaze was disconcerting, but then, so was everything else about the man.

"I found something for you to snack on," he said, offering her the plate. "Eat what you can. It'll help revive you."

"Thanks. I am rather hungry." She picked up the chicken leg and a paper napkin from the plate and began to eat. Halfway through, she paused to glance at him. "As soon as I eat, I'll be ready to leave. I don't want to keep you any longer than I already have."

He relaxed against the corner of the couch and crossed his boots out in front of him. The hems of his jeans were ragged and stained green with manure, while the pant legs were covered with dust and splotched with something dark, like blood. She didn't have to wonder if he was a hardworking man. It was evident from the burnt brown skin of his face, his calloused hands and dirty clothes. Even though Fort Worth was known as "Cowtown," and she'd seen plenty of men wearing boots and Stetsons walking the sidewalks, she'd never been close up to a man like him. His masculinity roared at her like a lion warning her to beware.

He said, "Don't worry about it. This is normal hours for me."

She took a deep breath and tried to concentrate on the chicken. "Have you had this clinic very long?"

"Twelve years," he replied. "It's my second home."

"Where's your first home? In town?" The questions came out of her before she could stop them. But thankfully, he didn't seem to mind.

"No. I live about twenty-five minutes from here. On Three Rivers Ranch."

"You have a ranch?"

"Partly. It's owned and operated by the Hollister family. My brother Blake is the general manager, but my mom has the final say-so over everything."

She shook her head. "Sorry. I'm being nosy."

"Not really." He gestured toward the mound of baby covering most of her lap. "When are you due?"

"About four weeks. That's why I'm...making this trip now, before there's a chance I might go into labor."

"I'm not an OB, but I'd say there's a chance you might go into labor sooner than that."

Her cheeks burned with hot color. "I just look that way because I'm— I've gained a little extra weight these past couple of weeks."

"No. I don't mean you look big. It's just the way you're carrying. But like I said, I'm not an OB."

No. But he'd probably seen plenty of pregnant animals, she thought. Oh, God, what was she doing here in this Arizona town, without one friend or acquaintance within a thousand-mile radius? Had she lost her mind?

No, you've not lost your mind, Roslyn. You've finally found it. Along with the guts to be your own person, live your own life, deal with your own mistakes.

"I should be fine until I get to California," she said, wishing she felt as positive as she sounded.

"You have relatives there?"

She didn't know a single person in California. She'd chosen that state because it was as far west as she could get from Texas. Also, her late mother, who'd originally lived in Redding, had left Roslyn a small house and piece of property there.

"No. I, uh, own a place in Redding."

"That's where you intend to settle?"

The chicken leg eaten, she put down the plate and he handed her the carton of yogurt. It was topped with blueberries, one of her favorite flavors.

"That's my plan. I've never been there before, but I've heard the town is pretty." Oh, Lord, why had she told him that? Now he was probably thinking she was completely irresponsible and chasing after pipe dreams. But this man's view of her wasn't important. Once she walked out of this clinic, she'd never see him again.

"Uh, I guess you're wondering why I'm traveling alone. Without a man."

"The question did cross my mind," he admitted.

Her gaze fell to his left hand. There was no wedding band on his finger. But given the man's occupation, he might choose not to wear one. He could be going home to a woman tonight. One that would be waiting for him with a smile on her face and love in her heart. Or was that sort of fairy-tale life even real? She wondered bitterly.

Dipping the spoon into the yogurt, she said, "I'm not married. And don't plan to be—at least, not anytime soon. The baby's father turned out to be a first-class jerk. So he's out of the picture. Completely."

He stroked a thumb and forefinger over his chin as

he regarded her thoughtfully. “That’s…unfortunate. The baby needs a daddy. There isn’t any chance—”

“No!” she blurted before he could finish. “Shortly after he learned I was pregnant, he signed away all his paternal rights to the child. Since then, he’s already moved on and married someone else.”

“Is that the way you wanted it? Surely making him pay child support—”

Shaking her head, she said, “I don’t need or want his money. Not that he actually had any money of his own, anyway. Besides, it’s more important to me to have him totally out of my child’s life.”

“I’m sorry it didn’t work out for you.”

The empathy in his blue eyes was more than her frazzled emotions could bear and she purposely dropped her gaze to the yogurt. “Well, better now than later.”

She began eating the yogurt, but it took effort to get each bite past her tight throat. She needed to get out of here, she thought—away from his perceptive gaze and unsettling presence.

After a long stretch of silence, he asked, “Have you already made reservations for a room in town?”

Focusing on the yogurt, she scooped out the last bite. “Uh, no. With it being early spring before vacationers hit the highways, I was hoping there would be plenty of vacancies.”

“I’m sure there will be. But I…”

When he failed to go on, she looked up. “What? Is there some place in town I shouldn’t stay?”

A faint smile tilted the corners of his lips. “No. That wasn’t what I was about to say. I was thinking it would be far better if you’d come home with me.”

Chapter Two

Chandler watched her eyes grow wide, her jaw drop. No doubt she was thinking he was some sort of pervert with a fetish for pregnant women. And he could hardly blame her.

It wasn't like him at all to invite a woman, a stranger at that, to spend the night at his family home. In fact, he'd never done such a thing. Sure, he'd taken home plenty of strays to nurture. But none of those strays had been the two-legged kind with pretty brown eyes and a shy smile.

"Home—with you?" she asked, her voice little more than a squeak.

"I'm speaking as a doctor, Roslyn. You've just suffered a fainting spell. I'd feel better if you weren't alone," he reasoned.

Her head began to swing back and forth. "I don't want to sound ungrateful, Mr. Hollister, but I don't know the first thing about you."

Lifting his hat from his head, he thrust a hand through his hair, then levered the hat back in place. His body was crying for food and a bed. But he was a long way off from either.

"Then I'll tell you a few things. The Hollister family has lived in Yavapai County for more than a hundred and seventy years and have owned and operated Three Rivers Ranch for just as long. My younger brother Joseph is a deputy sheriff for the same county and my sister, Vivian, is a park ranger over at Lake Pleasant State Park. Holt, another younger brother, has the reputation of being one of the best horse trainers in the southwest. And our mother, Maureen, is tougher than all her kids put together."

"Earlier, you mentioned your older brother, Blake. The ranch manager. I assumed he was the only sibling you had."

The surprise in her voice suggested she wasn't from a large family. He wanted to ask her if that was the case, but decided now was hardly the time.

"The Hollisters are a big family and we're all very close. I failed to mention I have another younger sister besides Vivian. Camille is living in the southern part of the state on one of our other ranches, Red Bluff. As for Three Rivers, Blake and his wife and three children live there, along with me, Holt and Mom. Vivian and her daughter used to live there, too, but she married recently and moved up to Camp Verde. So you see, there will be plenty of chaperones around the place."

"It sounds like you have a reputable family," she said after a moment. "And it's very hospitable of you to offer, but I'd feel like an intruder. A room in town will be perfectly fine."

"Not if you start feeling ill and need help. Trust me,

we have plenty of spare rooms in the ranch house. Along with a cook and a housekeeper. You won't be an intrusion. Far from it. Mom loves company. We all do."

She didn't reply and Chandler could see she was softening to the idea.

"I'm a stranger to you," she argued, but with far less enthusiasm. "For all you know I could be dishonest. A con woman or some evil person out to steal you blind."

Long years of working with the public had taught Chandler all about people. Sometimes it wasn't easy to see a person's true character. Other times all it took was a look into their eyes. He'd spotted plenty of emotions in Roslyn's brown eyes, but none of them had been close to sinister.

"You're not a con woman. You're alone and driving cross country, when you really should be home with your feet up," he added pointedly.

She winced at his last remark and Chandler decided then and there that she was most likely running from someone. If it wasn't the baby's father, then it had to be someone who'd been putting pressure on her. He hated to think a lovely girl like her had reached such a point in her life. Moreover, if he was smart, he wouldn't get involved with her, even for one or two nights. But Trey had hit the mark when he'd said that Roslyn seemed "kinda lost." And Chandler was a sucker for any animal or person who needed to find their way back home.

"Okay," she said, relenting. "I can see you're a gentleman. And it would be nice to really rest for a night."

Chandler was more than pleased at her answer. He was downright joyous. It was a reaction that had the sensible side of him silently cursing. What the hell was he thinking? He didn't have time to concern himself with the welfare of a pregnant runaway.

Still, Chandler couldn't keep a grin off his face. "Great. I'll get busy locking up the clinic and then we'll head on out to Three Rivers. While I take care of things you might want to visit the ladies' room. It's a long, bumpy ride to the ranch."

"Thank you. I appreciate your thoughtfulness."

He rose from the couch and offered her his hand. "Let me help you down the hall. I want to make sure you're steady on your feet before I leave you on your own."

She laughed. "If you're this attentive to your animal patients, you must have a whopping business."

The sound of her laughter was genuine and sweet, and eased some of the fatigue from Chandler's weary body. "Let's just say I can't remember a day when my schedule wasn't booked solid."

With her little hand wrapped around his, he helped her from the couch and purposely kept a steadying hold on her elbow.

"Are you dizzy?" he asked. "Do your legs feel sturdy enough to support you?"

"Oh, yes. I'm feeling much stronger now. I can make it on my own."

In spite of her insistence, he held on to her until they reached the door to the restroom. "Take your time," he told her. "And when you're finished, just wait for me up front in the waiting area."

Fifteen minutes later, Roslyn was sitting in the passenger seat of Chandler's truck. Her overnight case, filled with everything she needed for a night's stay, was sitting behind her, on the back seat.

"Sorry about having to leave your car, Roslyn, but part of the road to Three Rivers is rather rough. I promise it will be safe parked behind the clinic. There are security cameras all around the property and I've never had anything vandalized or stolen. Besides, I really don't think you're up to driving another twenty or so minutes."

Sighing, she rested her head on the back of the seat, while thinking how nice it felt to have this big, strong man handling everything for her. Even if it was just for this short evening.

"I'm not worried about my car. It's covered with tons of insurance. Besides, once I get to where I'm going I plan to trade it in for something more practical."

Roslyn had never wanted the Jaguar to begin with, but Martin, her father, had always insisted she had to drive a luxury car, not some cheap, middle-of-the-road compact. Otherwise, everyone would get the idea that the law offices of DuBose, Walker and Finley were going broke.

The idea had her silently snorting. If her father never earned another penny in his life, he'd still have an obscene amount of money stashed away in several banks. At the age of seventy he was still driven by his work, still obsessed with adding more power behind his name and seeing his fortune grow. But all the wealth or notoriety of Martin DuBose hadn't been able to buy his wife's health or to keep her from dying. Maybe someday he would realize that, she thought sadly. Perhaps one day he might regret the time he could've been spending with his wife and daughter, instead of in a courtroom.

Chandler said, "Everyone on Three Rivers has to be practical and drive a truck. After a while the rough road would shake a car to pieces."

"Is your home that remote?" she asked.

"We have a few neighbors, but there are miles in between all of us."

"I've always lived in the city." She peered out at what little she could see from the path of the headlights. Now and then they passed groups of mesquite trees, or a ragged patch of prickly pear. Otherwise the countryside appeared open and bare. "I do wish it was daylight so I could see everything. This is the first time I've been in Arizona."

"What do you think so far?"

"It's beautiful. And rugged. And wild."

He tossed a grin in her direction. "You left out hot. It gets as hot as hell here."

"Well, Fort Worth isn't exactly cool in the summer months." She'd not meant to come out with that, but what the heck. It didn't matter if Chandler knew where she was from. He wasn't going to broadcast the information.

"I noticed the Texas plates on your car. I've been trying to figure out what part of the state you might be from. I know it's so big that it's referred to in regions. North, south, east and west. I know some folks from South Texas, but they don't sound like you."

"That's right. I was born and raised in North Texas."

"But now you've left. Any regrets?"

"There will be places and people I'll miss," she confessed. "But no. No regrets."

"The Hollister family has been rooted here for so long I can't imagine living anywhere else."

"Your sisters must feel differently about that," she said thoughtfully.

"Well, love changes some people. Vivian is happy to live on the reservation with her husband. Now Camille is just the opposite. She's avoiding Three Rivers and Wickenburg because of a lost love. Or so she thinks."

A lost love. After Erich gave her an engagement ring and vowed his undying devotion, Roslyn had discovered he'd had been seeing other women. And with that shocking discovery, she'd believed she'd lost the one love of her life. But soon afterward, she'd realized she'd not lost anything. Rather, she'd escaped making a giant mistake with a man who knew nothing about real love.

"Men think with their heads. Not their hearts," she murmured more to herself than to him.

"Not always."

That brought her head around, and as she studied his profile, which was illuminated by the dash panel lights, she wondered if he'd ever trusted his heart to a woman and had it broken. She couldn't imagine him grieving over a broken romance. She could, however, imagine him having passionate sex without promises or strings attached.

"Are you married, Dr. Hollister?"

His short laugh was an answer in itself. "No. I barely have time to eat, much less see after a wife and kids."

For some inexplicable reason, his response saddened her. It shouldn't matter to her that this man was completely devoted to his career. "Well, it's good that you know your limitations."

"Hmm. I didn't know I had limitations. I just thought I was a busy man."

She forced herself to smile. "Sorry. You'll have to overlook me. I'm rather tired and things aren't coming out of my mouth exactly right."

"Well, just a few more miles and we'll be at Three Rivers. You can put up your feet and eat some of Reeva's good cooking."

Three Rivers. Each time he spoke the name it was like he was speaking of a place close to heaven. And for this one night that was exactly what she needed.

Fifteen minutes later, Chandler helped Roslyn into the house. After depositing her in a comfortable chair in the den, he went looking for his mother.

"Mom! Are you in here?" he called as he entered the large kitchen located at the back of the house.

Reeva, a tall slender woman in her early seventies with a long salt-and-pepper braid, was standing at the sink. She looked over her shoulder at him and frowned. "You're filthy and I'm shutting down the kitchen."

"Tell me something I don't know. Like where is Mom."

"She's down at the foaling barn with Holt. Better not go down there. You know that they'll put you to work and you don't look like you can stand on your feet much longer."

After working on Three Rivers for too many years to count, Reeva was crusty and cranky and very astute.

"Well, I'm going to have to call her up here because I've brought company home with me. And I'm not sure where to put her."

Reeva turned away from the sink to level a speculative glare at him. "Company? 'Her'? Have you brought a mama dog home with you?"

"No. This is a girl. A pregnant girl."

"Oh, Lord."

At that moment, the back door of the kitchen opened and Maureen Hollister entered the room. She was dressed in her usual work attire, which consisted of jeans, a long-sleeved shirt and cowboy boots. Her chestnut hair was slightly threaded with silver and pulled into a ponytail at the back of her head. At sixty-three, she was ageless and beautiful. She was also the glue that held the Hollister family together.

"Mom, thank God, you're here." He crossed the room and latched on to her arm. "You have to come with me. There's someone in the den waiting to meet you."

As he pulled her out of the kitchen, Maureen shot him a comical look. "Son, please tell me you're joking. I can't deal with company tonight! We've been branding calves all day and then one of Holt's mares, Tootsie, finally decided to give birth. And you know how he feels about that mare—you'd think his own child was being born. And—"

As they headed down a long hallway toward the den, Chandler pulled his mother to a halt. "Mom, I know it's late. And I know you don't need anything else to deal with tonight. But this girl—I just couldn't leave her there at the clinic. She needs rest and a woman's touch right now."

Her expression softened. "Oh, Chandler. Don't tell me you've brought home another stray."

Rather than trying to explain, Chandler gave his mother a tired smile. "Just come to the den with me."

When they entered the long room, Roslyn was sitting in an armchair with her back to them. But as soon as she heard their footsteps on the parquet floor, she rose to face them.

"Oh, my!" Maureen gasped. "You're a woman!"

"What were you expecting, Mom?" Chandler asked wryly.

She slanted Chandler a reproving look. "A dog with pups. Or a pregnant cat. Or a mother raccoon with her kits."

Leaving her son's side, Maureen rushed over to Roslyn and reached for her hands. "Hello. I'm Maureen Hollister," she said, introducing herself. "And you are?"

She smiled tentatively at his mother, "I'm Roslyn DuBose," she said, then cast Chandler a hopeless look. "And I'm sorry to interrupt your evening like this. I tried to tell your son that I'd be an intrusion, but he insisted on bringing me out here."

"Roslyn has been driving for long hours and she had a

little fainting spell," Chandler explained. "I thought she needed a quiet rest where someone would be around if she experienced another light-headed spell."

Roslyn continued to look apologetic and Chandler wondered if she was unaccustomed to asking people for help. Or maybe she simply felt awkward because she was among strangers. Either way, Chandler wanted her to trust him and his family. She needed to understand she was safe here.

She glanced at Maureen. "I could've gone to a motel, Mrs. Hollister, believe me."

Maureen immediately wrapped a supportive arm around Roslyn's shoulders. "Oh, honey, I'm so glad that you didn't. You're not in any condition to be staying by yourself. And company is always welcome here at Three Rivers. Did you bring a bag with you?"

Before Roslyn could answer, Chandler said, "I left it at the stairwell. I'll carry it upstairs. Which room?"

"The one across from Vivian's old room should be fine. I believe Jazelle freshened it up only a few days ago."

Maureen urged Roslyn forward and Chandler followed them out of the room and into another hallway that intersected with a wide staircase.

"Where's Blake and Katherine and the kids?" Chandler asked his mother as he picked up Roslyn's case and proceeded to climb the steps behind the two women.

"You never know what time it is, Chandler. It's late. They've retired for the night," Maureen answered. Then she explained to Roslyn, "My oldest son and his family stay on the third floor. They don't want the twins crying to disturb the rest of us."

"Hah! That's just an excuse to get away from all the noise we make down here," Chandler said jokingly, then tossed another question at his mother. "If it's so late, what's Reeva still doing in the kitchen?"

"Tessa and Joe and Little Joe came over for dinner, so Reeva made several extra dishes. I couldn't help her with the cleaning up because Holt called me down to the foaling barn." She glanced over at their houseguest. "Just a regular night on the ranch, Roslyn. Around here, you never know what's going to happen next."

On the second floor, they walked halfway down a wide passageway to a partially open door and entered a bedroom decorated in reds and browns and furnished with a queen-size bed and a large chest made of knotty pine.

Chandler said, "If the room looks masculine, Roslyn, that's because this used to be Holt's room. He moved downstairs a few years ago."

"During foaling season Holt is called out at all hours of the night," Maureen explained. "And as our resident vet, Chandler usually has to go with him."

"But even when it's not foaling season, Holt is coming home at all hours of the night," Chandler added with a sly chuckle.

Maureen let out a good-natured groan. "Chandler, our guest doesn't want to hear about the playboy of the family."

"No," he agreed. "She needs for us to get out of here and let her rest." He placed Roslyn's bag on the end of the bed.

His mother gestured toward a door in the far left corner of the room. "There's a private bath there with a shower. You should find plenty of towels and things. And if you get chilled in the night you'll find extra blankets in the closet. Now with that settled, are you hungry?"

"Thank you. I'm fine. Dr. Hollister gave me a chicken leg and a carton of yogurt."

Maureen rolled her eyes. "First of all, he's not Dr. Hollister around here. You'd better call him Chandler, or Doc, or Bones, or something like that, so we'll know who you mean. And secondly, a chicken leg and a bit of yogurt does not qualify as a meal. Especially when you're eating for a little one, too. I'll bring you some of the leftovers from dinner."

Chandler gave Roslyn a wink. "You probably ought to listen to her. She's had six of us."

"I'm not an expert on carrying babies, but by the time Camille was born, I felt darn close to it," Maureen said with a chuckle, then reached for Chandler's arm. "Come on. Let's leave Roslyn alone so she can get comfortable and ready for bed.

She tugged Chandler out the door and didn't let loose of his arm until they'd reached the landing at the bottom of the stairs.

Deliberately lowering her voice, she said, "Okay. What's going on? You've brought home plenty of things over the years, Chandler, but never anything like this!"

He glanced up the stairs just to make sure Roslyn hadn't followed and could hear them discussing her. "Well, it's pretty simple, Mom. When Trey and I returned to the clinic tonight, Roslyn's car was parked near the front of the building. Seems she'd gotten dizzy and pulled off the highway. I found her sitting inside the vehicle. She was a bit disoriented and while I was trying to question her, she fainted. As best as I could tell from dehydration and exhaustion."

"But where is she from? Who is she? Anyone you know?"

He shook his head. "She's from Fort Worth and apparently driving herself to California."

"The poor little thing," Maureen murmured with empathy. "No one was with her? Where's her husband?"

He grimaced. "She doesn't have one. And from what she tells me, she isn't going to have one. I think the baby's father turned out to be…uh, not the good guy she thought him to be."

"Oh. That's just awful."

"Well, I apologize for springing a guest on you this way, Mom, but I hated to think of her at a motel."

She released the grip on his arm and gently patted his shoulder. "No need for an apology, son. This is your home, too. Besides, you did the right thing. Roslyn might not even have the extra money for a motel room."

The two of them moved away from the landing and started toward the kitchen. As they walked together, Chandler said, "Wrong, Mom. Roslyn appears to be wealthy. She's driving a Jaguar and did you notice her clothing? I'm sure the pieces will have fancy labels inside."

"Hmm. I didn't notice her clothing," she admitted. "Did you ask her why she's traveling west?"

"No. It's none of my business. But from everything she's said, she's not going back to Texas. I'm guessing she's trying to get away from something or someone. Kinda like our Camille. In any case, I didn't think it would hurt to help her out for a night."

"Or two?" Maureen suggested slyly. "For the baby's sake."

Chandler glanced skeptically at his mother. "I don't believe she'll stick around for a second night. Unless you can persuade her—for the baby's sake."

Maureen gave him a clever smile. "All right, son. I'll give it a try."

He leaned over and pecked a kiss at the end of her eyebrow. “Thanks, Mom.”

She didn’t respond and by the time they reached the end of the hallway, Chandler was shocked to see a tear trickling down her cheek. Maureen Hollister never cried or rarely showed an emotional crack in her tough, ranch-woman armor.

Before she could shoulder her way through the swinging doors leading into the kitchen, he caught her by the arm. “Mom, I see a tear in your eye! What in the world is wrong?”

She blinked. “Nothing is wrong. I was just thinking.” Smiling wanly, she cupped her hand against the side of his face. “Have I ever told you just how much you remind me of Joel?”

A tight knot of grief twisted in the middle of Chandler’s chest. “Oh, Mom, don’t compare me to Dad. It isn’t fair. I could never be the man that he was.”

“Not exactly. But you are like him in so many ways. And that’s a comfort to me, Chandler. Always remember that,” she said gently, then her mood instantly brightened and, smiling, she urged him through the swinging doors. “Let’s see what Reeva has left for you in the warming drawer. You might have to share it with your little Texas stray.”

She was a stray all right, Chandler thought. But she didn’t belong to him. Like any other stray he’d picked up in the past, he could afford to offer her food and a temporary home. But he wasn’t about to risk offering her a piece of his heart.

Chapter Three

By the time Maureen returned with a tray of food Roslyn had taken a quick shower and dressed in a pair of yellow cotton pajamas and matching robe.

"If you'd like to prop yourself up in bed and eat that's fine," Maureen told her. "You won't hurt the spread if you spill anything."

"That's okay," Roslyn told her. "I'll just sit here in the armchair. It's very comfortable."

She settled herself in the soft green chair and allowed Maureen to place the tray on her lap. On it, there was a plate filled with braised beef ribs, a small bowl of *charro* beans, two flour tortillas and a dish of apple-crumb cobbler. Just looking at the food caused her half-empty stomach to growl with need.

"I thought I wasn't hungry. But looking at this makes me feel like I'm starved," Roslyn admitted. "Thank you for bringing it up, Mrs. Hollister. I, uh, never expected you to wait on me like this."

"I'm Maureen to you. And it was no problem bringing the meal to you. I hope you like it. Reeva is a wonderful cook. We've had her in the family for years." She took a seat on the foot of the bed. "You don't mind if I stay while you eat, do you?"

"Why no. It's nice to have company," Roslyn admitted. "For the past two days I've pretty much been talking to myself. Traveling alone gets a little lonesome."

Maureen smiled with understanding, and not for the first time since she'd met Chandler's mother, Roslyn was totally awed by the woman. Not only was she beautiful and strong, but she was also warm and genuine.

"I know what you mean. I drive up to Prescott fairly often. Which is not that far, but it's much nicer when someone makes the trip with me. Chandler tells me you're from Fort Worth."

Roslyn nodded as she swallowed a piece of the tender beef. "I was born in Fort Worth and have lived there all my twenty-five years."

"Twenty-five. Oh, dear, at your age, I'd been married for four years. Blake was about two years old then and I was pregnant with Chandler. That's been a long time ago."

Roslyn's mother, Geneva, had been thirty years old before she'd married Martin. Two years later, she'd given birth to her one and only child, Roslyn. She'd been a fragile woman who'd never had the strength to show any sort of independence. All of her life, she'd stood in Martin's shadow and lived only to please him. Roslyn couldn't imagine this woman knuckling under to anyone.

"That's hard to imagine," Roslyn admitted. "You look so young."

"You're too kind." Chuckling, she glanced down at

herself. "I'm not exactly looking my best. I did have on a dress for dinner, but then duty called at the foaling barn."

"Do you have lots of horses and cows on the ranch?" Roslyn asked curiously.

Maureen nodded. "Holt can tell you the exact number of horses. Probably somewhere between a hundred and fifty to a hundred and seventy-five head. Blake keeps count of the cows. They number in the thousands. That's counting the ones down at Red Bluff and on our grazing land near Prescott."

"Oh, it sounds like Three Rivers Ranch is a large business."

"Very large," Maureen said. "It takes a lot of hands to keep everything going. Along with me and Blake and Holt and Chandler."

Roslyn tore off a piece of the tortilla and dipped it into the spicy beans. She'd never tasted anything quite so delicious. Or maybe going twelve hours without eating had left her so famished a piece of burnt toast would have been tasty.

"And your husband?" Roslyn asked. "What part does he do on the ranch?"

Maureen cleared her throat. "Joel died a few years ago—from a horse incident. Before that, my husband was the general manager of the ranch. After Joel died, Blake took over the position. Believe me, at that time my oldest son didn't want to step into his father's boots and I couldn't blame him. It's a heavy responsibility. But as the oldest and most qualified, he had to…well, become the head of the ranch so to speak."

Roslyn wasn't expecting to hear anything like this from Chandler's mother and the fact that this family hadn't gone without their share of heartache made her feel a kinship with this woman.

"I'm so sorry, Maureen. I shouldn't have asked. I just assumed that—"

Roslyn waved a dismissive hand to halt her words of apology. "Don't be sorry. Dear God, I've been a blessed woman. I was given many wonderful years with Joel and I have six beautiful children to show for it. So tell me about you. Do you have family back in Fort Worth?"

Roslyn couldn't see that holding back the truth from this woman would do any good. She'd be leaving here in the morning. Even if Maureen decided to take it upon herself to call Martin DuBose, something Roslyn sincerely doubted the woman would do, there was no way her father could get here that quickly. Unless he chartered a plane.

"I have a father and a paternal aunt. My mother died five years ago of leukemia."

Maureen shook her head. "Twenty years old is too young to lose your mother. But we don't have a choice in those matters, do we?"

The gentle, understanding expression on Maureen's face made Roslyn want to lay her head on the woman's shoulder and weep until she could weep no more.

"No," Roslyn said, her voice thick with emotion. "And it was very hard seeing her go through years of treatments and suffering. But I…really miss her. Especially now with the baby coming. And my father—he's very condemning about my choice not to marry the baby's father. You see, he's from an older generation. And the DuBose name is important to him in the social circles of Fort Worth and Dallas. I've pretty much become an embarrassment to him. But… I can't let that bother me anymore. My only concern is my baby. And making sure it has a nice, loving home."

"And that is exactly what you should be concerned about," Maureen said firmly. "When is your baby due?"

"In four weeks. I told Chandler that's why I was traveling now. I need to get to where I'm going before the baby is born."

Maureen left her seat on the bed and came to stand in front of Roslyn. "I don't want to sound bossy, or have you thinking I'm trying to tell you what to do. I'm sure you've already heard plenty of that from your father. But as a mother, I feel like I should advise you that you shouldn't put too much stock in your due date. Babies, especially first ones, can be unpredictable. You really need to be settled now. With someone around to help you in case you do go into labor."

Not for anything did she want Maureen to see how alone and anxious she'd been feeling about the future. Yes, she had plenty of money for housing and living expenses, she had plenty of medical insurance to cover her and the baby's hospital care. Yet none of that could make up for having a loving man at her side.

"You're right, Maureen. And I was hoping to get away from Fort Worth last month so I would have more time. But Dad always seemed to be watching my every move. Finally, three days ago, he flew up to Wyoming on business, so I managed to make my getaway."

"You didn't want him to know you were leaving?"

Roslyn grimaced as she stirred a spoon through the beans. "No. There would've been an ugly scene. He would've done everything in his power to stop me. You see, he wants me to think I'm incapable of taking care of myself or my baby. He wants me to stay dependent on him."

"So he can more or less control your life," Maureen said sagely. "Some parents have a hard time letting go."

Roslyn could've told Chandler's mother that her father had more issues than just letting go of his child. He'd controlled every aspect of his wife's life. Even after Geneva's death, he'd gone against her wishes to be buried next to her parents in California. Instead, he'd thought it more fitting to do it his way with a lavish funeral and burial in Fort Worth. But Maureen didn't need to know about the DuBose family problems. It was bad enough to admit she'd had to resort to running away in order to escape the man.

Sighing, she looked up at Chandler's mother. "Forgive me, Maureen. I shouldn't be telling you any of this. And it…sounds so petty. Except…it isn't."

Maureen laid a comforting hand on Roslyn's shoulder. "I'm glad you can talk to me. Just remember that family problems don't get solved in a day. Tomorrow things will look brighter, I promise. Right now just concentrate on finishing your meal and I'll pick up the tray in a few minutes."

She gave her shoulder another pat, then started out of the room. When she reached the door, Roslyn called to her.

"Maureen, thank you, again. And please thank Chandler for me. He was very kind to help me the way he did."

Maureen gave her a wink. "He may not look it, but Chandler's a big softie. I'll give him your thanks."

She gently closed the door behind her and Roslyn, lost in thought, lowered her fork and looked around her.

Three Rivers Ranch house was not like anything she'd expected. Instead of a Spanish-style hacienda, it was a three-story wood frame. The inside had a rustic feel, while at the same time being warm and comfortable.

Judging by her surroundings, Roslyn could see the Hollisters didn't lack for money. Yet if she'd met Chandler or Maureen on the street, she would've never guessed they were wealthy. Unlike her father, who never failed to flaunt his riches.

Stop it, Roslyn. Quit thinking about your father. Quit blaming or judging him for being rich. His need for wealth and high regard from others are his own problems. Not yours. You're out of it now.

But was she really? Roslyn questioned the grim voice going off in her head. True, these past two days she'd been on the road, she'd been out from under his thumb. But would she ever be able to move past the emotional prison he'd kept her and her mother in for all those years? She had to think so. She had to believe that somewhere, someday, she would meet a man who would love her just for being her and together they'd make a home filled with warmth and happiness.

The next morning, as soon as Chandler arrived at work, he expected Trey to start badgering him with questions about Roslyn. But it wasn't until after they'd dealt with the colts on the Johnson ranch and were driving back to the clinic that Trey finally brought up the subject.

"So what happened with your visitor last night?" Trey asked. "Did you finally get her sent on her way?"

Roslyn hadn't been *his* visitor, but correcting Trey on that point would be useless. "I guess you could put it that way. I took her home to the ranch."

Trey shifted slightly in the seat and gawked at him. "The hell you say!"

Chandler very nearly laughed. "That's right. In her condition she was in no shape to be left alone at a hotel. I thought it best to let Mom take over."

"Oh. Guess that was a surprise for Maureen."

"Mom is always ready for anything." Chandler glanced

at his watch. He'd left Three Rivers at five this morning. More than four hours had passed since he'd operated on the five colts for Mr. Johnson and headed back to Wickenburg. By now he figured Roslyn was champing at the bit to get on the road again. In fact, he wouldn't be surprised to learn she'd already caught a ride into town with one of the hands and drove off in that sleek little Jaguar she considered impractical.

"Is she planning to stay around Wickenburg?" Trey asked.

Chandler couldn't foresee that happening, even if a part of him wanted it to. Which didn't make one iota of sense. She was far too young for him, not to mention pregnant with another man's child. Even if he was in the market for romance, he didn't need to set his sights on a woman like Roslyn. Still, it would be nice if she stayed around until the baby was born. Just so he'd know the two of them were okay.

"No. She says she's headed for California. She has property there."

"Well, she sure is a—"

"Pretty little thing," Chandler said, finishing for him.

Trey shot him an annoyed look. "Now how did you know I was going to say that?"

"Because you said it last night and you tend to repeat yourself."

"Well, I wasn't wrong about that, was I? I mean, I'm not a man who goes around looking at pregnant women, but she was nice. Kinda soft and sweet. You know what I mean?"

Chandler hadn't thought about the softness or sweetness of a woman for a long time. It was something he tried not to think about. Sure, in his younger years he'd done the dating merry-go-round. He'd even had a couple of relationships he'd believed would turn into something more serious. But with both of those women, his job and the ranch had gotten in the way. Since then he'd decided to keep his mind on his work and away from romance.

"Yeah, Trey. I know what you mean." He glanced over at the tall, raw-boned man, who usually had an affable smile on his face. "Just why haven't you gotten yourself a wife, anyway? You ought to have a wife and three kids already."

Trey looked at him and sputtered, "Wife and kids! Hell, you're six years older than me and you don't have a family. Why are you picking on me? Just think about it, Doc. If I had a wife she probably wouldn't like it if I got the urge to go to the Fandango on a Friday night. She probably wouldn't like me going on any night. And that might cause big problems."

Chandler chuckled. "Yeah, big problems."

At the intersection of Highways 60 and 83, Chandler made a left. After two more miles the clinic came into view. As soon as he turned into the parking area and drove past the building, he glanced to the spot where he'd parked Roslyn's car last night.

"Well, what do you know, it's still there," he murmured more to himself than to Trey.

"What's still there? What are you talking about?"

He braked the truck to a halt beneath a pair of Joshua trees and killed the motor. "Roslyn's car. It's still there. I thought she'd be gone by now. I guess Mom must have done some fast talking."

Trey winked at him. "Whose idea was that? Yours or your mom's?"

Chandler shook his head. "I don't have time for your nonsense. This place is running over with horse vans and cattle trailers. Go see what's going on at the barns. If it's anything you or Jimmy can't handle, tell them they'll have to wait their turn."

"Got it, Doc."

Trey hurried away in the direction of the barn and Chandler headed to the clinic. As he walked, he pulled out his cell phone and checked his messages. Near the top was a new one from his mother.

Roslyn is staying one more night.

He slipped the phone back into his pocket and as he entered the back door of the clinic, he very nearly collided with Cybil. The tall, middle-aged woman with a mass of frizzy blond curls had worked as his main assistant with the small animal patients for the past five years. Chandler relied on her to keep things moving smoothly and somehow she managed to do it.

"Good thing there's a smile on your face, Doc. The waiting room is jammed this morning and Mr. Fields is already grumbling about missing his morning coffee at Conchita's."

Mr. Fields was in his eighties and believed his age gave him the right to talk as loudly and sharply as he wanted, no matter where he happened to be or whom he was addressing. "Don't tell me that dog of his has swallowed another piece of plastic."

Chandler started walking down the hallway to his office and Cybil made a U-turn to follow him.

"No. It's his cat this time," she answered. "A facial cyst. I've put her and Mr. Fields in examining room two."

In his office, Chandler pulled on a lab coat and hung a stethoscope around his neck. "What's in room one?"

"A dog with a nose full of prickly pear spines. And room three is a rooster. Something is wrong with his eye."

"While I deal with the cat, sedate the dog," he ordered, then glanced questioningly at Cybil. "And a rooster, you say? It's not a fighting cock, is it? If it is, I'll have to report it to law officials."

"No worries there. It's a pet."

"That's a relief. I don't have time to spend my morning talking with a Yavapai deputy. Even if the deputy turned out to be my brother Joe."

Grabbing a pen from his desk, Chandler crammed it into the pocket on his lab coat and motioned for Cybil to follow him down the hallway.

As the two of them strode rapidly toward the examining rooms, Cybil said, "What's the deal with the fancy car, Doc? Surely you're not planning to drive it back and forth to the ranch."

He should have realized the staff had spotted Roslyn's car parked behind the building and immediately begun to speculate.

"Not mine. It belongs to a visitor—at the ranch," he said, deciding that was the easiest way to explain things. Besides, he could count on Trey to eventually spread the gossip about a young pregnant woman fainting in the parking lot.

Later that afternoon, at the ranch house, Roslyn sat in an armchair watching Katherine and Blake's twins, Andrew and Abagail, toddle precariously between the couch and a nearby love seat.

"The twins only took their first steps a couple of days ago. Now they both think they have walking mastered," Katherine said with a laugh. "Nick, our older son, didn't walk until he was a year old. So I wasn't expecting these two to start racing around at nine months."

Roslyn said, "I've been reading about the different

stages of a baby's life and what to expect about teething and walking and that sort of thing. But I guess nothing is cut and dried."

Katherine chuckled again. "Don't count on anything being normal."

The babies weren't identical, but they did resemble each other. Both were dressed in yellow rompers and shoes with soles solid enough for walking. They each had dark curly hair, gray-blue eyes and dimples in their chins. It was obvious that Katherine adored them and from what she'd already told Roslyn, their father, Blake, thought the world revolved around the babies.

As Roslyn watched them play, she couldn't help but think how different things would've been if Erich, her ex-fiancé, hadn't turned out to be a philandering, money-grubbing creep. By now, the two of them would have been married and instead of preparing to give birth alone, she'd have a husband by her side. But given the revelation of the man's true nature, she was very lucky not to have him in her life. In fact, she thanked God that she'd discovered the real Erich before their elaborate wedding plans had taken place.

Shaking away those grim thoughts, she smiled at the twins. At the moment the babies didn't want to stray very far from their mother, but Roslyn figured that would soon change. "Your babies are beautiful, Katherine. I wish mine was here already."

"Don't worry. He or she will be here soon enough. Then you'll be wondering if you'll ever sit down for more than five minutes at a time." The amused expression on the woman's face turned empathetic. "I suppose you'll be starting to work after the baby comes. I imagine some of your friends have already warned you that's the hardest part of being a mother. I'm a secretary three days a week for a school superintendent in Wickenburg and I love my job. But leaving the babies is still tough. Thankfully, Jazelle takes care of them while I'm at work. She's wonderful with them and I don't have to worry."

"Oh, I thought Jazelle was the housekeeper."

"Jazelle is the housekeeper, along with assistant cook, maid, errand runner, nanny and everything in between."

If Roslyn had chosen to stay in Fort Worth, her father would've hired the most expensive nanny he could find for his grandchild. And it wouldn't stop there. He'd eventually be telling Roslyn how to dress the child, where it should go to school, what friends it should have, and the sort of career and education it would need to be successful. The control would never end. Just as it hadn't ended with Roslyn, until three days ago, when she'd packed everything she could into the Jaguar and driven away from the DuBose palatial home.

"I'm hoping that when the time comes I can find a trustworthy nanny. But I won't be going to work until the baby is a few months old. To be honest, I've not decided what I want to do in the way of a job." As soon as she finished speaking, her cheeks grew hot with embarrassment. "Oh, Lord, that makes me sound like a ditzy schoolgirl."

"No. You don't sound ditzy. More like you don't have everything quite planned out yet. But I'm sure you'll get there," Katherine gently replied.

Roslyn sighed. "To be honest, Katherine, I've never had the opportunity to have a job. My father would never allow it."

Katherine frowned. "I've never heard of such. But I guess he had his reasons."

Roslyn refrained from rolling her eyes. "I did graduate from college with a degree in business, but that was more or less to pacify my father. He thought his one and only child should have a college education. He just never intended to let me use it. A wealthy man doesn't need the women in his family to help make a living. That's his mind-set."

Katherine shook her head. "Strange that we've both had difficult fathers. Except mine was on the opposite end of the spectrum from yours. He was an alcoholic and by the time I reached high school I had to find odd jobs to help the family stay afloat. My mom pretty much made all the household income. But Dad died a few years ago. And now that I look back on it, the work and the scraping by made me a stronger person. I only wish that Dad could've seen the twins. He would've adored them."

This woman was wishing her difficult father was still in her life, while Roslyn was wishing she'd never see hers again. The realization made her feel small and spoiled and ungrateful, yet on the other hand, she had to believe she'd made the right decision to leave her father's house. For herself and for her baby.

"I'm thinking your father probably can see the babies," Roslyn said softly.

Katherine nodded. "I'm thinking so, too. And back to your father not wanting you to hold down a job—doesn't he realize there are plenty of other reasons for a woman to work, other than making money? For instance, my mother-in-law, Maureen. Blake has repeatedly told her that the ranch can afford to put on another hand to take her place. But she'd never agree to such a thing. And frankly, I'm glad she feels that way. Working keeps her young and gives her a purpose."

Early this morning, when Roslyn had come downstairs for breakfast, most everyone had already eaten and they were all hustling and bustling to get to their jobs. She'd not seen Chandler anywhere and then she'd overheard Reeva telling Maureen that he'd left the house at five and she'd sent a sack of breakfast tacos with him.

I barely have time to eat, much less see after a wife and kids.

Last night, when Roslyn had asked Chandler whether he was married, she'd hoped his response had been exaggerated. She'd even wondered if he might even be using his job as an excuse to remain a bachelor. But she was beginning to see he'd been telling the truth. His veterinary practice consumed his time.

Thoughts about the man were still drifting through her mind, when Andrew toddled in her direction. Roslyn held out her arms to encourage the baby to come to her, but his attention was instantly distracted by a tiny object on the floor. The baby plopped on his rear and reached for the fuzzy piece, but before he could poke it into his mouth, Katherine left the couch and grabbed her son's fist.

"Andy, that's nasty," Katherine told the baby. "Let Mommy have it."

The toddler allowed his mother to pull the object from his grip, then immediately regretted handing it over. He puckered up and began to whimper as his mother dropped the ball of hair and lint into a small trash basket.

"Sorry about that, Kat," Jazelle said as she entered the den carrying a tray loaded with an insulated coffeepot and two cups. "It's probably a wad of horse hair. I swept this room earlier, but Holt came traipsing through here a while ago wearing his chaps."

"Don't worry about it, Jazelle," Katherine told her. "If there's one tiny speck on the floor, the babies will find it."

The housekeeper set the tray on a nearby wall table

to keep it out of the twin's reach. "I made decaffeinated coffee so you could have a cup, too, Roslyn."

Roslyn gave her a grateful smile. "Thank you, Jazelle. All of you here on the ranch have been so thoughtful and caring that you're making me feel like a princess. Honestly, I'm all over my fainting spell. In fact, I should have left today. But your mother insisted I stay another night."

"Of course you need to stay another night," Jazelle told her. "Kat and I don't get many female visitors out here. And Reeva loves it when she has someone new to cook for."

Jazelle poured the coffee, adding cream to Roslyn's before she handed the cups to her and Katherine, then disappeared from the den. Once she was gone, Roslyn rose from the chair and, carrying her cup with her, began to amble around the long room.

The wooden parquet floor possessed a warm brown patina and was dotted here and there with cowhide rugs. The tongue-and-groove walls were painted a sandy beige and covered with enlarged photos depicting various scenes of ranch life. At one end was a huge rock fireplace with a wide hearth. Presently the screen was closed, but Roslyn could easily imagine a huge crackling fire and the family gathered around, relaxing on the leather furniture that was scarred and softened from years of use.

"This house has so much character," Roslyn commented. "Nothing seems to be new and I love that about it."

"After more than a hundred and seventy years, a house develops a life of its own, I suppose. This one certainly has its own personality. The first time I ever saw this place I was only a young girl. And even then, I was awed by the rooms. The way it all looked and felt and smelled. Nothing much has changed since then, except the people who live and work here have all aged. And then, of course, Mr. Hollister—Joel—is gone. Losing him is still hard for the family to take."

Stepping onto the fireplace hearth, Roslyn picked up a photo from the mantel and gazed thoughtfully at the group of men circled around a branding fire. She could easily recognize Chandler standing by his brothers Blake and Holt, whom she'd met this morning. Along with them was a younger, dark-haired man, she guessed to be their brother Joseph. Another, older man was squatted on the heels of his boots as he held a branding iron to the low flames. He very much resembled Chandler.

"I'm guessing the man holding the branding iron in this photo is Mr. Hollister," Roslyn remarked. "Chandler looks like him."

"You're right. That's Joel. What I remember about him was his kindness, like Chandler. And like Holt, he was a big teaser." Katherine left the couch and joined Roslyn on the hearth. "I don't expect Chandler or Maureen mentioned any details to you about Joel's death. It's not something any of them want to talk about."

"Last night Maureen told me her husband had died from a horse incident," Roslyn replied.

"Well, that's basically the way the sheriff's department ruled it. Death by accident. But none of Maureen's children believe that's what actually happened to Joel. There are too many reasons to debunk the accident ruling. They all think someone killed Joel, then staged the horse dragging to make it look like an accident."

A chill rushed over Roslyn as she carefully placed the photo back on the mantel. "Are you saying the family believes someone actually murdered Mr. Hollister?"

Katherine nodded. "They've slowly been finding a few

clues. But so far there's still too many missing pieces to convince law officials to reopen the case."

"What about Maureen? Does she believe her husband was murdered?"

Katherine shook her head. "We used to think she believed it. In fact, she was in complete favor of Joe and his brothers searching for the truth. But these past several months, she seems to have had a change of heart about the matter. She tells us she wants to quit dwelling on it and put the whole matter behind her."

"You're frowning, Katherine. And I guess I don't understand why. Wouldn't putting it all behind her be a good thing for Maureen? I mean, it's such an ugly, depressing idea."

"I agree. It is ugly. But Maureen has always wanted to know the truth of what happened to her husband. Something has happened to cause a change in her."

"How awful for her," Roslyn murmured ruefully. "And here I've been feeling sorry for myself because my father wants to tie a ball and chain around my ankle. All I can say is that Maureen must be an extraordinarily strong woman to have gone through so much sorrow and still come out smiling."

"She's definitely an iron lady," Katherine agreed.

Roslyn would've liked to ask her lovely new friend more questions about the Hollister family, but at that moment both twins began to fuss. As Katherine went to tend to her babies, Roslyn gazed once again at the photo.

When she'd lost her mother, it had torn out her heart. She'd felt as though she'd lost everything. She hated to think what Mr. Hollister's death had done to Chandler. Last night he'd seemed so kind and genuine. Even now she could recall the way the corners of his lips had tilted with amusement and the way his blue eyes had sparkled like sunlight on water. Being near him had made her feel good and protected and deep-down warm. The feeling was like nothing she'd experienced before and if she was being totally honest, she was still here on Three Rivers Ranch because she wanted to see the man again.

Chapter Four

After the chaotic schedule of the morning and early afternoon, Chandler hadn't expected to make it home by dinnertime, but somehow the large animal patients had tapered off and he and Cybil had managed to clear out the last of the small animal cases by regular closing hour.

Now as he jammed the tails of a white shirt into his blue jeans and brushed back his damp black hair, he almost didn't notice the exhaustion that was seeping into his bones. After all, how could he think about being tired when he was going to see Roslyn again?

He'd reached the bottom of the stairs and was heading toward the den when he heard a male wolf whistle behind him.

Glancing over his shoulder, he watched his brother striding purposely toward him. With thick, rusty brown hair and an inch or two less than Chandler's six foot two, Holt was lean and as tough as a boot. He also attracted women like flies to honey.

"You look dapper tonight," Holt stated with a clever grin. "You even combed your hair. Guess you're wanting to make an impression on our little houseguest, huh?"

Chandler let out a good-natured groan. "Don't go there, Holt. The woman is pregnant. Or did you fail to notice?"

Holt's grin grew wider. "I noticed. What's the deal with her, anyway?"

Chandler looked at him with wry disbelief. "Don't tell me you haven't already asked Mom."

Holt put on his innocent face. "No. There are some things a guy doesn't want to discuss with his mother."

Chandler barked out a short laugh. "Sure, Holt. Since when did you turn into a sensitive guy?"

With the entrance of the den fast approaching, Holt grabbed him by the arm to stop him. "Oh, c'mon, Chandler, level with me. What's she doing here, really?"

Annoyed that Holt was using up time Chandler could be spending with Roslyn, he said, "She needed a bit of help, that's all. Don't worry. She's not out to steal us blind."

"That thought never entered my mind. But there are other ways a woman can cause a man trouble."

"You ought to know."

"Damn it, Chandler! I'm serious."

With a placating grin, Chandler placed a hand on Holt's shoulder and urged him forward. "Thanks for your concern, little brother. I realize I'm not as experienced as you when it comes to women, but I think I can manage to keep myself safe."

"Okay. Be flip. But one of these days you're going to get that big ol' soft heart of yours broken."

Holt's prediction pulled a chuckle from Chandler. He wasn't in one place long enough for a woman to get any kind of hold on him. "And one of these days all the women in Yavapai County are going to discover that you don't have a heart."

Holt shot him a pained look. "Ouch. After being insulted like that I'm going to need a double shot of bourbon before dinner."

"Just be sure you don't get into the expensive whiskey Mom saves for Sam," Chandler warned. "She'll have a fit."

Holt chuckled craftily. "You got that wrong. Sam would be the one to have a fit."

The two men entered the den and Chandler instantly spotted Roslyn sitting on the couch with Maureen. She was wearing a pale yellow dress with a sash that tied in a small bow beneath her breasts. The soft fabric draped over her belly, emphasizing the fact that she was in the latter part of her pregnancy. Part of her shiny hair was pinned to the crown of her head, while a few tendrils fell against the back of her neck. She looked utterly feminine and completely charming, and as he moved deeper into the room, he found he couldn't tear his gaze away from her.

"Chandler! This is a pleasant surprise!" Maureen exclaimed as she spotted him working his way to the couch.

He bent to kiss his mother's cheek. "Good evening, Mom. For once we managed to close the clinic before eight o'clock at night."

"I'm happy to hear it. And you've arrived just in time." Maureen stood and gestured for Chandler to take the cushion she'd just vacated. "You can keep Roslyn company while I go to the kitchen and check on Reeva."

Since when did Reeva need checking on? Chandler came close to asking his mother the question, but at the last moment decided there was no need to look a gift horse in the mouth.

"My pleasure," Chandler said. "That is, if Roslyn doesn't mind sharing the couch with me."

As Maureen moved away, Roslyn smiled up at him. The warm expression melted something deep in the middle of his chest. The feeling caused Holt's prophecy to whisper through Chandler's head, but he promptly shook it away. When it came to matters of the heart, Holt was clueless.

"Hello, Chandler," she said. "I'd love for you to join me."

He eased down beside her and crossed his ankles out in front of him. "Has Jazelle passed around any drinks yet?" he asked, then before Roslyn could answer, he spotted the housekeeper. "There she comes now. I hope she remembered you can't have anything with alcohol."

Roslyn laughed softly. "You do sound like a doctor, Doc."

Her happy mood was uplifting and he figured he would burst if he didn't smile back at her. "There's something about mothers-to-be that brings out my protective nature," he explained. Then he asked, "You have rosy cheeks tonight—are you feeling stronger?"

"I'm feeling wonderful. Everyone here at the ranch has been so kind. And they won't allow me to lift a finger. Much more of this and I'll get to thinking I'm a princess instead of pregnant."

"Everyone treated Katherine like a princess, too, while she was carrying the twins. And for good reason. She suffered with nausea during the first trimester."

"I think Katherine could still use a little extra pampering. She's been chasing the twins around all afternoon."

Chandler glanced around the room. "I don't see her or Blake. They must have gone out tonight?"

"Your brother and sister-in-law are upstairs putting the twins to bed," Jazelle said, answering his question. "They should be down shortly."

Jazelle lowered the tray in front of them and Chandler pointed to a long-stemmed glass half-full of dark wine. "Is that for me?"

"Just for you, Doc. And the pink glass with ice is for Roslyn. Reeva mixed up ginger ale, cherry syrup and lime juice. It's one of her specialties."

"Sounds yummy. Thank you, Jazelle," Roslyn told her.

Chandler handed the glass with the special concoction to Roslyn and Jazelle moved on to Holt, who'd sunk into an armchair across from them.

"Your bourbon and Coke, Holt," Jazelle told him. "The best stuff."

Holt gave her an appreciative grin. "I think we'll keep you around, Jazelle."

"Thanks, Holt. It's good to know my job is secure," she said drily.

Holt laughed and Jazelle went on her way.

Chandler glanced over to see Roslyn had been taking in the playful exchange between Holt and the housekeeper. "Have you met my brothers yet?" Chandler asked her.

"I met them both early this morning at breakfast. Holt was telling me about one of his mares foaling a colt last night. And I didn't know that the word *colt* specifically meant the baby was male. He explained to me that the females are fillies and the males are colts. And then Blake explained the difference between heifers and steers."

"Our lessons for the day," Holt said with a grin. "And

no, we were both nice. We didn't call Roslyn a greenhorn."

Chandler looked at her and wondered what she'd been thinking today about his home and his family. Probably that everything here on Three Rivers seemed big and rowdy and a little too coarse for her taste. Yet the sparkle in her brown eyes seemed to imply she was enjoying herself.

What difference does any of that make, Chandler? The woman is here on a momentary basis. And once she leaves here you'll never hear or see her again. Just keep that in mind before you let those brown eyes make you a little gaga.

Chandler sipped his wine and tried to shake away the chiding whispers in his head. "Fort Worth is known for being horse and cattle country. I'm surprised you don't know anything about ranching," Chandler told her.

"My father is a corporate lawyer," she explained. "And we've always lived in the city. On occasion, I see cowboys around town, but that's about as close as I've ever gotten to a cow or horse. Dad has handled a few cases in the past for wealthy ranchers, but I never met them."

"All the more reason you should hang around Three Rivers for a while," Holt suggested with a grin. "You can learn plenty about ranch life around here."

She appeared to be searching for a reply when Holt's phone made a chirping noise.

Frowning, he pulled the phone from his shirt pocket. "Excuse me, you two. This message might be important."

While Holt scanned the text, Chandler turned his attention back to Roslyn. "Did you venture outside today and look around the place?"

She nodded. "I went as far as the front porch and the back patio. It's all very beautiful, Chandler. And from the front porch, you can see for miles. It's very different from where I lived. We didn't have a front porch for sitting and the only thing you can see when you're standing there are houses around us. Don't get me wrong. They're all lavish homes with perfect lawns, but it's not like seeing the rugged mountains and stretches of desert."

Chandler wondered what she thought about the stark contrast between Three Rivers and her home back in Fort Worth. Obviously, she'd lived a privileged life, but he also got the feeling that she'd been missing something very important. Otherwise, she would still be there instead of heading to somewhere she'd never seen in California.

"The ranch looks more isolated than it actually is. Joseph and his wife and baby live only a few miles from here on the Bar X Ranch. I wish they were coming to dinner tonight. You would've enjoyed meeting them. Tessa is twenty-seven now, I think. Only a couple of years older than you, so I'm sure you'd find things in common to talk about."

"Katherine mentioned to me that Tessa is originally from a ranching family in Nevada. And how she traveled down here to Arizona on her own," she replied. "So I guess in a way we do have something in common."

"Well, I'd say you're both young, adventurous women." With an emphasis on the *young* part, Chandler thought. Roslyn was eleven years younger than him. Some folks would think that many years would create a giant chasm between a man and a woman. Yet strangely, he didn't feel the gap.

Across from them, Holt slipped the phone back into his pocket and bolted back the last of his drink. "Excuse me, you two. I have to go to the foaling barn."

"Do you need me?" Chandler asked.

Shaking his head, Holt rose from the chair. "Thanks,

brother, but I think I can handle this. Tell Mom I should be back in time to eat. And save a seat next to Roslyn for me," he added with a wink.

"She wants to enjoy her dinner, brother, not listen to your nonsense." Chandler grinned, then shooed him onward. "Let me know if you need me at the barn."

Holt left the den by way of the French doors that opened on to the back patio. Once he was out of sight, Roslyn said, "From what Jazelle and Katherine told me, Holt is crazy about horses."

"And women. And in that order. The horses come first with Holt and then the women."

"Hmm. You two men do seem to love your animals," she said, an impish smile softening her words.

"It's a cowboy thing," he jokingly explained. "Did you leave a pet back in Fort Worth?"

Her expression abruptly sobered. "I've never had a pet of any kind. Dad always said they were nasty and he didn't want them around the house."

With each little revelation she made about her life back in Texas, Chandler was patching together a picture of her father and it wasn't exactly a pretty one. "What about your mom? She didn't like animals, either?"

She sighed. "Mom died five years ago. She liked animals, but she was the sort that always went by Dad's rules. No matter how unduly strict they were. I had friends who had cats and dogs, though, and one had a rabbit named Moe. He was especially sweet."

Like Chandler, she'd lost a parent, too. But unlike him and his siblings, they'd been left with a parent who made sure each of her children felt loved and happy. In that way, he'd been blessed.

"I'm sorry about your mother," he said gently. "Were you two close?"

Her eyelids lowered as she took a sip from her glass, but not before Chandler had spotted a flash of pain in her eyes. “She was…very special. She was everything to me.”

The tiny break he heard in her voice was like a punch to his gut. His father had been his hero. Losing him had jerked something out of Chandler that he couldn’t define or explain. How did a man explain a hole that refused to heal?

“Did she have an accident?” Chandler asked.

“No, she suffered through a long battle with leukemia. After she died, the house didn’t seem like a home anymore. Not that it ever was a home like—” she gestured around the room “—you Hollisters have.”

“Thank you. But I don’t want you to be misguided by what you’ve seen last night and today. Things aren’t always rosy around here. We have our problems—like all families do.”

“Everyone has problems.” She gave him a wan smile. “But I have the feeling that you Hollisters deal with your problems together.”

And she didn’t have that togetherness. Was that what she was trying to tell him? That, except for a rigid father, she was all alone?

Well, hell, Chandler. The answer to that is pretty obvious, isn’t it? She’s alone and intent on traveling to any place she thinks she can make herself a happier place to live.

The monologue going off in his head was too sad to ponder and he joked in an effort to lighten the moment. “Yes, put that way I guess we do. But the disagreements can get loud at times.”

She chuckled. “I’m willing to bet as kids that you and your brothers got into some pretty rowdy scuffles.”

“Well, Blake was never a hothead and Joseph was the

baby of us boys, so those two were rarely in on the fisticuffs. But Holt and I would go at it. When that happened Dad would usually let us fight to the finish. But Mom was a different matter. She'd break us apart and send us to our rooms to let us stew over our behavior." He glanced up just in time to see Maureen entering the room. "Speaking of Mom, here she comes. Let's hope she's going to tell us dinner is ready. I'm so hungry I could gnaw on a piece of raw macaroni."

Laughing, Roslyn laid a hand on his forearm. "I wouldn't advise that, Chandler. You might choke."

He tried not to notice that she was touching him. After all, it was just casual contact that meant nothing. And yet the warmth of her hand sent an unexpected spurt of pleasure through him.

"Dinner is ready," Maureen called out.

Chandler rose from the couch, then offered his hand down to Roslyn. "Let's go eat, shall we?"

Roslyn took his hand and once he'd gently pulled her to her feet, she didn't hesitate to wrap her arm through his. The gesture reminded him that he was more than an overworked veterinarian. He was a man who'd gone a very long time without the company of a woman.

"I'm looking forward to every bite," she assured him. Then, using her free hand, she patted the top of her belly. "And I'm sure Baby is, too. Years from now, I'll be sure and tell him that he once had dinner on a real Arizona ranch."

And years from now Chandler would still remember this beautiful pregnant stranger, who'd stopped on his doorstep long enough to carve a little niche in his heart.

Later that evening, after everyone retired to the den for coffee and dessert, Chandler and Blake were discussing vaccination schedules when Maureen crossed the room and clamped a hold on Chandler's arm.

She said, "Sorry to interrupt you two, but I need to speak with you, Chandler. Alone, in my office."

Blake waggled his eyebrows in a teasing manner. "Better watch out, brother," he warned. "Mom's sounding like a school principal."

He winked at his brother. "If you hear me yelling, better come to my rescue, Blake."

"Oh, bull," Maureen scolded the two men. "I don't have my dander up. At least, not tonight. I just want Chandler's ear for a few minutes."

"Sure, Mom. Lead the way."

He followed his mother out of the den and down the wide hallway to a study that used to serve as his father's office. After Joel's death, Maureen had taken over the chore of balancing the books for the ranch house, along with the bunkhouse expenditures. As for the bulk of the paperwork associated with the business end of the ranch, Blake and his secretary handled that monumental task in his office, which was located down at the ranch yard.

"I'm sorry to pull you away from your brother," Maureen said as the two of them entered the office. "I realize you two don't get enough time with each other. So I'll try to keep this short."

Most of the space inside the long, narrow room was taken up with a large mahogany desk with an executive chair, two heavy wooden chairs, a set of filing cabinets and shelves jammed with an array of books and folders. While his father had been alive, the room had always held the scents of leather and strong coffee. But now that his mother had taken over the space, that had changed to a mixture of lemon furniture polish and juniper.

She switched on a banker's lamp on the desk, then

looked at him pointedly. "Just how much do you care about Roslyn DuBose?"

The blunt question had Chandler staring at her in disbelief and he tried not to stutter. "What are you talking about?"

"I'm talking about our houseguest. I want to know what you think about her."

For his mother's sake, he bit back the curse word on the end of his tongue. "Great balls of fire, Mom! I only met her last night."

"Yes. And you brought her home with you."

"Because she needed help," he reasoned.

"There are plenty of people around Wickenburg who need help. You don't bring any of them home with you."

Chandler thought he'd quit blushing years ago. Leave it to his mother to bring a shade of red to his face.

"All right, Mom, I get your point. But when I first discovered Roslyn in her car, the situation was a bit urgent. All in all, I didn't want her going off on her own and having another fainting spell."

Her sigh was a sound of impatience. "I'm hardly chiding you about this, son. I'm trying to gauge your feelings about her, that's all."

Why was his mother persisting about *his* feelings? Where Roslyn was concerned he didn't have any. Except for caring about her general well-being.

Liar. Liar. You've enjoyed every second you've spent in Roslyn's company. All day today, she's occupied your thoughts. You've been dreading her leaving and wondering how you're going to forget her once she's gone.

The reproachful voice in his head made him want to groan out loud. "Look, Mom, Roslyn is fine now—at least, physically. And you heard her say during dinner that she plans to leave in the morning. So she'll be out of your hair soon."

The grimace on Maureen's face said he'd clearly disappointed her. "Chandler, I ought to give you a swift kick in the ass."

His eyebrows shot up. "Why? What have I done?"

"You're assuming that I want Roslyn to leave."

Chandler made an openhanded gesture. "Don't you?"

She frowned at him. "Absolutely not. The girl needs us. In so many ways."

Chandler's mind began to spin. "Oh, now, Mom, I don't know exactly what you have on your mind, but Roslyn isn't your responsibility, or mine."

She eased a hip onto the corner of her desk and pierced him with a thoughtful gaze. "You're right. She isn't. At her age and single, she isn't anybody's responsibility. But I thought…well, we have plenty of extra room. And Reeva throws out enough food to feed three or four more people. It wouldn't hurt to ask her to stay on with us for a while—at least, until she has the baby."

Stay until she gave birth? But that would be days, weeks even, Chandler thought. By then she would be starting to feel like family. By then, the tender, protective feeling he got whenever he was near her might turn into something more serious. Something that could wind up being very painful.

"Mom, she's a stranger. We don't know her. Not really. Maybe this is what she had planned all along. Maybe she'd heard about the Hollisters and deliberately parked at the clinic last night just as a way to get her foot in the door."

Her expression suddenly sheepish, Maureen nodded. "God forgive me, but those same concerns crossed my mind. That why—this morning I did some checking up. Or let's just say I had someone do some checking for me."

Chandler was surprised. Normally his mother was far too trusting. "You didn't call her father directly, did you?"

"No. Nothing like that. I just wanted to make sure that Martin DuBose existed and that Roslyn's story was true."

Just thinking that Roslyn might not be truthful made Chandler feel like a heel. "And?"

"Everything she's told us checked out. And from what my source told me, the old man is known as a real cold codger."

It was a relief to hear Roslyn had been honest with them, yet it was sad, too. She didn't deserve that kind of father.

He said, "Well, obviously she isn't lacking money. I believe right now she's trying to get over the mistake she made with the baby's father. And she's longing for a place to call home. That's what I'm thinking."

"A home is exactly what she needs for herself and the baby—whenever it arrives." Her expression rueful, she asked, "Did you know her mother died?"

"Yes. She told me." Chandler shook his head. "And I can see, when she mentions her father—there's a look on her face that is so full of anguish and resentment I know it can't be an act."

Maureen smiled gently. "There's a look on your face, too, whenever you're near her."

Chandler let out a short laugh to cover his awkwardness. "Mom, you're all wrong. Sure, she's pretty. And I like her—a lot. But that's all. For Pete's sake, she's going to have a baby."

"That fact only makes her more precious."

"And she's years young for me. Besides, I'm already

hooked up with the clinic and the ranch. No. Don't be matchmaking for me. It won't work."

She let out a long sigh. "Okay, Chandler. No matchmaking. All I ask is that you take Roslyn aside and convince her that she needs to stay here on the ranch. At least, until after the baby arrives and she gets back on her feet."

Why in hell was his mother doing this to him? Didn't he have enough on his plate to deal with? Hadn't she stopped to notice that he was stretched to the breaking point?

Thrusting a hand through his hair, he tried to tamp down his frustration. "Me? Why me? She thinks you're wonderful. You're a mother figure to her—she'll listen to you."

Maureen shook her head. "You're the one who first found her and took care of her. You're the one she trusted enough to allow you to bring her out here to the ranch. You're the one she feels connected to."

Maybe his mother could see all of that, but Chandler sure couldn't. Hardly thirty minutes had passed since Roslyn had announced at the dinner table that she'd be leaving tomorrow. That didn't sound like the woman felt a connection to him or the ranch.

But maybe she was leaving because no one had asked her to stay. The thought rambled through his head as he began to move aimlessly around the room.

"I didn't realize this was going to put such a strain on you, son," she said cunningly. "Perhaps it would be better if I get Holt to speak with her. He knows exactly what to say to a woman."

He paused to stare at her. "Like hell! Holt doesn't know how to talk to a woman like Roslyn!"

"What do you mean, *like* Roslyn?" she asked sagely.

"She's young and pretty. Holt knows all about those kind of women. And every other kind, I might add."

Chandler wondered how it was that his mother always knew exactly which buttons to push to make her children comply with her wishes.

"Is it really that important to you that Roslyn stay? I mean, you have more than you can deal with as it is."

Shrugging, she said, "Well, with Camille living down at Red Bluff and Vivian and Hannah gone to the reservation, I'm feeling a little lost for my daughters and granddaughter. It would be nice to have Roslyn and the baby around. And maybe, in turn, we can help her get things righted in her heart."

There was no way he could argue that point. Especially when the whole family had been concerned about the gradual change taking place with their mother. A change that had nothing to do with her daughters and granddaughter moving out. No, they all believed it had something to do with Joel's death and uncovering the truth.

If Roslyn and the coming baby would be a pleasant distraction for his mother, even if only for a few weeks, then he was all for it. And perhaps in the long run, a stay here would help Roslyn, too.

"All right, Mom. I'll talk with her. But I'm sure not going to make any promises. I think she has going west on her mind."

"Then you need to convince her that Arizona is west enough," Maureen said brightly, then straightened to her feet. "Come on. I've already had Jazelle light a fire out on the back patio. You can take Roslyn out there to have your private talk."

"Mom, I've already warned you about matchmaking. I don't need a fire to get the point across to Roslyn."

Taking Chandler by the arm once again, Maureen urged him out of the office. "Good grief, son, you have matchmaking on the brain. This has nothing to do with that. I just want Roslyn to feel warm and relaxed when you bring up the question about her staying."

His mother was maneuvering him. That much was obvious. And normally Chandler would've already dug in his heels. But this wasn't Maureen's usual behavior. She never stuck her nose in any of her children's personal business, unless they asked for her help or guidance. And in the end, what would it hurt to comply with her wishes? After all, he was a grown man. His mother could just do so much leading.

Chapter Five

The flames in the fire pit sent flickering fingers of orange and yellow light across the patio and lit Chandler's features with a golden hue. Roslyn had no idea why he'd invited her out here. Especially when she figured he had to be weary from the long workday he'd put in. No doubt the comfortable furniture in the den would be more relaxing to him. Whatever his reason for this outdoor excursion, she was glad he'd made thc suggestion.

The fire warmed the cool desert air and when she gazed beyond the patio toward the ranch yard, she could see the clear night sky was stamped with thousands of stars. It was a beautiful night and her last night here. She wanted to savor every moment of it before she said goodbye to the ranch and the friends she'd made here.

"Are you warm enough?" he asked. "I can stoke the fire if you're feeling chilled."

"I'm perfect," she assured him. "The fire feels great."

He was sitting next to her on the wide rock ledge that

surrounded the fire pit—close enough for her to reach over and touch him. If she was inclined to do such a thing. And, oh, yes, she was feeling very inclined. All through dinner, she'd thought about touching him in ways that had caught her completely off guard.

After learning of Erich's unfaithfulness, she'd felt so angry and betrayed that she'd been certain it would take years before she'd ever feel any sort of desire for a man. She'd believed it would take an emotional earthquake before she'd be able to trust any man. Yet, from the moment she'd met Chandler, she'd felt an instant connection. A belief that she could put her trust in him. It was crazy.

"I have a confession to make, Roslyn. I brought you out here to the patio for a reason."

His remark cut into her tumultuous thoughts and she looked at him with blank surprise. "A reason? Oh. You must have wanted to get me out of the den so that Maureen could have a private word with the rest of the family."

He shook his head. "No. She and I already had private words in her office. And...well, to be frank, we were discussing you."

Jolted, she turned her knees so that she was facing him head-on. "What about me? Did she—?" Her mouth was suddenly so dry she couldn't swallow. "Has she contacted my father?"

He frowned. "Mom wouldn't do anything like that. None of us would. Not unless you asked us to."

Relief pushed a long breath from her lungs. "I'm sorry. It's just that... I can't deal with him. Not now. Maybe never."

"You sound very bitter, Roslyn."

"I'm sorry," she said again. "I'm sure you and your family think I'm an ungrateful brat. But believe me,

Chandler, I didn't leave Fort Worth on an impulsive whim. Ever since Mother died, I've wanted to leave. There was nothing there left for me. Not emotionally, or in any other way."

"That was five years ago," he stated. "Something must have kept you there."

She shrugged. "Hope, I suppose. I kept hoping that with Mother gone, Dad might actually need me around to fill the void. That didn't happen. He has his work. But then Erich started showing interest in me and we started dating. After that, things got much better."

"Your father approved of the union?"

Her laugh was short and dry. "Erich was from an old, respectable family, who'd been friends with my parents for many years. When we eventually got engaged Dad was thrilled. In his eyes we were the perfect match. And for the first time I could ever remember, he actually acted as though he was proud of me."

"What happened when your engagement ended?" he asked.

She sighed. "Dad went from being proud to blaming me for the whole breakup. According to him, if I'd made myself more desirable, Erich would've never turned to other women."

His blue eyes made a slow survey of her face and Roslyn wondered what he was thinking. That she was a real mess? That her father had probably been right about her inability to hold on to her fiancé? Oh, Lord, it was all so embarrassing.

"That was a terrible thing to say to you, Roslyn. You needed his support, not recriminations."

"Well, I didn't expect anything more from him. But that's enough about my problems. You brought me out here to talk and I'm rambling." She gave him the cheeriest smile she could muster. "So what did you need to speak with me about?"

He didn't immediately answer and she got the impression he was uncomfortable. The idea bothered her greatly. Last night, when he'd walked up to her car window, she'd found a friend. She didn't want that to change.

"Your plans for leaving tomorrow," he said finally. "Mom wants you to stay put. Here on the ranch—with us."

This was the last thing she'd expected to come out of his mouth and she stared at him in disbelief.

A half grin cocked up one corner of his lips. "Does that surprise you?"

"No. It stuns me." Without a shred of warning, tears filled her eyes and when she spoke again, her voice was a choked whisper. "Maureen is too kind for her own good."

"Mom's always had a big heart. But she's not a pushover. She doesn't offer an invitation like this unless she really means it."

Rising to her feet, she walked aimlessly to the edge of the patio and stared out at the night sky. Only minutes ago, she'd been thinking how Three Rivers was so beautiful and peaceful. She felt protected and wanted here, something she'd not felt since her mother died. To spend more time with this family would be a dream come true. On the other hand, she wasn't at all sure it would be wise. Especially when she looked at Chandler. He made her feel things she shouldn't be feeling. And think about things that had nothing to do with the plans she'd made for her and her baby's future.

Glancing over her shoulder, she saw that he was watching her and waiting patiently for a response. She drew in a deep breath and let it out. "I honestly don't know what to say, Chandler. This is all so sudden and unexpected."

He left the fire pit and came to stand next to her. Roslyn tried not to notice the alluring male scent emanating from his clothes and the way his muscular body towered over hers. Everything about the man reminded her that she was a woman. One with an empty hole in her heart.

"I'm sure you weren't thinking about staying on here," he said. "But—"

"It's not a good idea, Chandler," she interrupted, while purposely keeping her gaze on the sky. "Your mother is a very busy woman. As are the rest of you. I'd only be a nuisance."

"You're hardly a child that needs to be watched over," he countered. "Aren't you really worried that you'll be bored out of your mind staying out here?"

His question took her by surprise and she swung her gaze to his skeptical face. "Bored? Are you joking? Compared to the DuBose home this place is as busy as the Dallas-Fort Worth airport terminal. Something always seems to be going on."

"Yes, but it's not like the city, where you can go shopping or find all kinds of entertainment to keep you occupied."

"That sort of thing gets old quick. Is that what you think my life consisted of back in Fort Worth? Shopping and entertainment?"

His smile was sheepish. "The thought might've crossed my mind. What did you do with your time back in Texas?"

"Well, like I told Katherine, Dad would never allow me or Mother to work. But I still managed to make myself useful by helping plan charity events for children's causes, doing volunteer work at the girls club and tutoring a few high-school students with their math. That sort of thing."

"All of those are commendable tasks," he said. "But

you're at the age where…well, you could've been building a career for yourself. Or maybe you never wanted one."

She grimaced. "I never thought too much about it, Chandler. To go against Dad would've made my mother very unhappy. And with her being so ill, the issue of my future didn't seem very important. After she died, I finished getting my college degree in business. But it was mostly just to have a piece of paper to show I wasn't a complete dunce."

"I don't believe anyone would want to label you a dunce," he said wryly. "And congratulations on the degree. I hope one day you'll decide to use it."

She looked away from him and swallowed hard. "Yes, from now on my life is going to be different. I might have lost my father, but I've gained my freedom. You can't imagine what that feels like."

His hand was suddenly lying upon her shoulder and the warmth from it spread all the way down her arm and into the tips of her fingers. "You know, staying here for a while, until the baby comes, will give you time to adjust to all these changes you're going through. And we'll all be around to help—if you need us."

Us? Did that mean him, too? The mere idea that he cared about her well-being made her feel more special than she'd ever felt in her life. Even more than the moment when Erich had slipped a diamond engagement ring on her finger. How could that be?

"Do you—? Would you mind if I stay?" she asked haltingly.

A wry smile twisted his lips. "Why would I? Both of my sisters are living away now and Mom needs a stand-in daughter to nurture. Whatever makes her happy makes the rest of the family happy."

So he wanted her around for his mother's sake, she

thought. Well, that was certainly better than not wanting her around at all.

"Put that way, I can hardly refuse," she said. "But I'll tell you true, Chandler, it's hard for me to believe that you and your family want to take on a burden like me. I'm overwhelmed by your generosity. Really, I am."

The hand on her shoulder lifted and he grazed the knuckles gently against her cheek. "I don't want to hear you say you're a burden. Ever again. Hear me?"

"If you say so."

"I do. Say so." He curled his arm around her shoulder and urged her toward the French doors leading into the den. "Come on, let's go back in and tell Mom you're going to stay. She'll be very happy."

Walking along beside him with his arm curled protectively around her, she almost felt as if she belonged here. "You know what, Chandler? It makes me very happy, too."

During the next week Roslyn drove her car from the clinic to the ranch and moved all her things into the upstairs bedroom she'd been using since the first night she'd arrived on the ranch. Maureen had offered her a larger room with a sitting area, but Roslyn had assured the woman she didn't want to change. The coziness of the smaller room appealed to her. She particularly loved the rustic pine furniture and the padded window seat, where she could sit and watch the busy comings and goings of the cowboys down at the ranch yard.

In the meantime, Katherine had managed to get Roslyn an appointment with the OB, who'd delivered her and Blake's twins nine months ago. Yesterday she'd kindly accompanied Roslyn into Wickenburg to meet with the doctor, and after a thorough exam, he'd pronounced both her and the baby healthy. According to him, she should plan on going into labor in another four weeks. Give or take a few days.

Which meant Roslyn had a month, maybe more, to live on the ranch before she'd need to pack up and head on to California. And during that time, she intended to enjoy every second spent with the Hollister family.

Now, as she sat on the front porch of the ranch house, she was on her cell phone, trying to convey to her best friend back in Fort Worth exactly why she was somewhere in Arizona, soaking up the spring sunshine and doing her best to put her father and Erich Parker far behind her.

"You can't imagine how good it is to hear your voice, Roslyn. It's been a week and a half or more since you left and I haven't heard a peep from you until this very moment. I'll be honest, I almost contacted your father, just to see if he knew where you were."

Roslyn groaned with frustration. "Oh, Nikki! I specifically asked you not to say a word to him and you promised!"

"I said *almost*. I didn't. But look, Ros, I had a right to be worried. We've been friends since…well, our kindergarten days together. And I'm not one bit happy about you leaving. If you'd wanted to get out of your father's house that badly, you could've moved in with me. Or gotten an apartment somewhere in the city. Or even moved to Dallas. God knows your father would never go over there looking for you. He sees that city as the devil's playground."

Roslyn pinched the bridge of her nose. She'd been dreading making this call to her old friend, because she knew beforehand that the other woman was going to put up an argument. Still, Nikki had been her closest friend since they were small girls. Roslyn couldn't just dismiss her from her life.

"Well, you needn't worry any longer," Roslyn told her.

"I'm in a beautiful place with a very nice family. And I intend to stay here until a couple of weeks or so after the baby is born."

"Exactly where are you? And who are these people? Can you trust them?"

"I'm in Arizona—in the desert. And as to the people I'm living with, they're a well-known and respected family. I wouldn't be here if I couldn't trust them," she answered evasively.

"That's not telling me much," Nikki grumbled. "And I've been trying to call you for days! Don't you have cell service there?"

Roslyn grimaced. "As soon as I left Fort Worth I turned off my old phone and didn't make any calls or texts. I didn't want my father to be able to track my route."

Yesterday, when she and Katherine had been in Wickenburg, she'd purchased a new phone with a different number, so she wouldn't have to worry about her father tracing her through connecting tower pings. Nor was she ready to tell Nikki her exact location. Her friend was well-meaning and would never intentionally go against Roslyn's wishes, but she often spoke without thinking. If she let Roslyn's whereabouts slip to mutual friends, the information would eventually make it to her father.

"I thought all of Arizona was desert," Nikki said.

Roslyn smiled. "Geography never was your best subject."

Her friend chuckled. "Funny, isn't it? I barely know where to find Texas on the map and I end up working for a travel agency. Good thing all I have to do is make reservations."

"It's a very good thing," Roslyn joked, then asked, "So how are things going with you? Still dating Randy?"

There was a long, pregnant pause before her friend

finally answered. "No. He decided to enter the marines. He'll be leaving for California in a few weeks."

"And he didn't ask you to go along with him?"

Nikki sighed and Roslyn could picture the other woman frowning and absently twining her long red hair around her finger. "He did. But I told him no."

Roslyn gasped. "But why, Nikki? You're crazy about the guy? Why let him slip away?"

Another sigh sounded in Roslyn's ear. "I don't want to leave Mom. Not in her present state of mind."

"My dear friend, it's not your fault that your father decided to divorce your mother and go live on the east coast with another woman."

Nikki was silent for another long moment and then she said, "No. But if I left Mom, too, I'm not quite sure she could handle being totally alone. Maybe later when she's had time to adjust to the loss."

Later would probably be too late for Nikki to make the life she'd wanted with Randy, but Roslyn was in no position to give her friend that sort of grim advice. Not when she'd already had a broken engagement and an unexpected pregnancy with a man who'd turned out to be a liar and a cheat.

After visiting with Nikki a few more minutes, she ended the call and was about to walk back into the house, when she noticed a truck like Chandler's coming up the long driveway. Pausing, she watched the dusty vehicle stop near the front gate and the busy doctor climb to the ground.

This past week, she'd scarcely seen the man. Once in the early morning, he'd been exiting the house by way of the kitchen. On that occasion he'd paused long enough to tell her good-morning and that he had to hurry to the clinic to deal with an emergency. Then one night she'd gone to the kitchen for a glass of milk and found him eating his supper, while going through a stack of medical records. He'd looked very tired and though he'd invited her to take a seat and join him, she'd not wanted to hang around and make a nuisance of herself.

But today was different. Today he looked full of energy as he trotted up the wide steps.

"Well, hello, Roslyn," he said with a broad smile. "How's the little mother-to-be?"

Blushing, she smiled at him and tried to ignore the way her heart was dancing a silly little jig in the middle of her chest. "I'm fine, thank you. You're home very early, aren't you? There's still a few hours of daylight left," she commented.

He chuckled. "There'd better be. My receptionist crossed out this late afternoon so I could get away from the clinic. There are times I have to work for the ranch and this is one of them. Blake wants me to check on two different herds of cattle. Some of the hands have reported a few of the cows having pink eye."

"Are you talking about the same sort of pink eye that humans have?" she asked.

"No. It's different. Bovine pink eye isn't contagious to humans. But if left untreated in cattle it can easily spread through the whole herd." His gaze traveled up and down the length of her. "Say, you're wearing jeans. And boots, too! Nice!"

Her cheeks turned a deeper pink at his compliment. "Thank you. I got them yesterday when Katherine and I went to town." She smoothed a hand over the loose blue gingham shirt covering her baby bump. "I thought the jeans would be practical for wearing here on the ranch. And she talked me into the boots to go with them."

"Boots are a necessary footwear on a ranch," he said

with a grin, then slanted her a thoughtful look. "Are you busy right now?"

She laughed softly. "Busy? What would I be doing? Each time I offer to sweep or pick up, or help in the kitchen, I'm told to sit down. I'm beginning to feel like a sitting hen."

His grin turned sly. "Then how would you like to go with me? The road out to the grazing range is fairly smooth and you won't have to get out of the truck unless you want to."

She had to stop herself from jumping up and down with excitement. "Oh, I would love to go. I've only walked down to the ranch yard twice since I've been here and that's as much of the ranch that I've had a chance to see."

"Then it's about time you saw more of it. Can you be ready to go in five minutes?"

"Sure."

"Then meet me in the kitchen. The truck we'll be taking is parked out back."

"I'll be right there," she promised.

After a quick trip to the ladies' room and grabbing a light jacket from the closet, Roslyn hurried down to the kitchen, where she found Reeva loading Chandler down with a thermos of coffee and a plastic bag filled with homemade cookies.

"We're not going on a picnic, Reeva," Chandler told her. "Seeing a cow with pink eye doesn't exactly give a man an appetite."

"I'm not worried about you, Chandler. This is mainly for Roslyn. She's eating for two, you know. And this is her last month, the time when the baby is putting on weight. She needs plenty of calories. And I made the coffee decaffeinated just for her."

Chandler shared a knowing smile with Roslyn as he

ushered her out the back door. “I’m sure you’ve guessed by now that Reeva mothers all of us.”

“It’s pretty obvious,” Roslyn agreed. “Maureen told me that Reeva has a grown daughter and one grandchild in California, but that she rarely sees them.”

“That’s right. Her daughter, Liz, is one of those people who wants everyone to believe she was born at the top of the social circle. It embarrasses her that Reeva works as a cook. In fact, Reeva says her daughter tells her friends that her mother works as a secretary.”

“How sad. Sounds like this Liz has misguided priorities,” Roslyn replied. “Especially when Reeva is such a wonderful person. I honestly don’t know where she finds all her energy. She never quits working. But then, neither do you.”

With a hand on her elbow he helped her down a set of short rock steps, and kept the steadying hold on her arm as they walked to a white truck with the 3R brand painted on the door.

“I wouldn’t know what to do with myself if I wasn’t busy,” he said.

“How about take a nap?” she suggested impishly.

He laughed and she laughed with him and for the first time since Roslyn had left her home in Texas, she felt the heaviness in her heart lift and fly away with the warm desert breeze. It felt so wonderful to be with this man, she thought. His company made her almost forget that she would soon be a single mother and that the man who’d proposed to love her had not really loved her at all.

“You’re very funny at times, Roslyn,” he said, as he helped her into the work truck. “I like that. As for the nap, I wouldn’t know how to do that, either.”

He shut the door, then went to the back of the truck and let out a loud whistle. She turned just in time to see him lowering the tailgate and two yellow short-haired dogs leaping into the truck bed. After he'd closed the gate, he joined her in the cab.

"I've seen several dogs around the barns. Some were this color and others were spotted with longer hair. Are they all pets? Or working dogs?"

"I guess you could call them both. But mostly they're working dogs. This pair that's going with us today are Black Mouth Curs and very good at rounding up cattle. I don't expect I'll need them to work today, but they like to go with me. They're very sweet and social, so you can pet them if you'd like. They won't take off your hand. The spotted dogs you've seen around the ranch yard are Australian shepherds. I raise and train them to work cattle, also. That is, when I have the time."

He opened the console between the seats and dropped the thermos and cookies into the storage space. "I'll put these in here so they won't end up rolling under our feet. You can get them out whenever you'd like."

"I honestly don't want to ruin my appetite," she told him. "Reeva is cooking something special. Polish sausage and macaroni and cheese."

Laughing, he glanced in her direction. "That's not special. That's plain ol' comfort food."

She chuckled. "Maybe that's why I love it."

He started the truck and reversed out of the small parking area behind the house. As they drove past the ranch yard, she noticed a group of mounted cowboys, riding away from the ranch.

"Where are they going? To round up cattle?"

"Not at this time of day. They're probably going to ride fence line to make sure there are no posts or wires down. It's a never-ending job."

"Can't they do that job in a vehicle?"

"A few cross fences can be checked from a vehicle. Most of the ranges, however, are too rough for vehicles to travel over. And Mom has always kept Dad's policy of not using ATVs or helicopters on the ranch."

"Why? Just to keep with the older tradition of doing everything on horseback?"

"Well, the Hollisters are all about tradition. But the main reason is that loud machinery puts undue stress on the cattle and can even cause them to be injured. Ninety-five percent of the time, a cowboy can ride his horse quietly into a herd and the cattle will remain still and calm. Try doing that with an ATV and they'll stampede in every direction."

"Oh, I wasn't aware of that." She looked at him and smiled. "I guess you can tell I'm very ignorant about ranching."

"Would you like to learn?"

"I would like to learn," she answered, then added, "This will probably sound silly to you, but before I came here to Three Rivers, I never really got acquainted with being outdoors and I've discovered that I like it. There's something soothing about being surrounded by nature. It's given me a different perspective about life."

"I think that's very true."

He shoved the floor shift into a higher gear, but still maintained a slow pace. The narrow road they were traveling was dirt and wound randomly through clumps of blooming sage and tall saguaros. She'd never seen such wild and rugged countryside, yet its enchanting beauty couldn't draw her attention completely away from Chandler.

Beneath his gray Stetson, his black hair gleamed like a crow's wing, while his blue eyes were as striking as the azure sky. The Western shirt hugging his shoulders and torso was fashioned of khaki material and looked as if it had been tailor-made to fit his muscular build. His presence was so big and masculine it seemed to fill up the entire cab of the truck.

"Do you think you might look for an outdoor job once you get settled in Redding?" he asked.

Reining in her wandering thoughts, she focused on his question—one that had been plaguing her ever since she'd learned she was going to be raising a child without the help of its father.

"I haven't thought that far ahead yet. The main reason I was going to Redding was because Dad doesn't know anything about the property I own. So he wouldn't know to look for me there. The place was one secret my mother kept from him. Because she knew he'd find a way to take the place away from her, or me."

"I see."

Did he really? She doubted it. Because it was hard for anyone to understand that kind of behavior.

"Well, I feel confident they'll be some sort of job there for me," she said as cheerfully as she could. "One thing for sure, I'm not trained to do any sort of outdoor job. My college degree is in business. Dad picked out the subject. He thought that was more fitting for a woman."

He glanced in her direction. "What would you have chosen for yourself, Roslyn?"

She pondered his question for a moment and realized how cocooned her life had been until she'd started dating Erich. And even then, she probably wouldn't have gotten engaged if it hadn't been for her father pushing the issue.

"I don't know. That's awful to admit, isn't it?" She turned slightly toward him. "It's hard to explain, Chandler, but when you grow up with someone else choosing everything for you, then your imagination and dreams never really have a chance to flourish. Each time I tried to plan something on my own, it was always interrupted or changed. I realize now just how spineless a person I've been. For years I did everything my father's way. And then when Erich came along I did everything his way."

"And now?" he asked.

Straightening her shoulders, she said, "Now I'm going to follow my own convictions. I'm going to think for myself and my baby."

"I'm glad to hear that, Roslyn."

Wondering if he was making fun of her, she glanced at his rugged profile. Yet there was no amusement to be found on his face and the fact filled her with simple joy. More than anything, she wanted this man to see her as smart and strong and capable.

"You know, Chandler, it's almost staggering to think there's a whole new world out there and I can do and be what I want. I'm not sure what that is yet. Except that I want to be the best mother I can possibly be. And the love I give to my child won't come with chains."

He reached over and gave her hand an encouraging squeeze and Roslyn was swamped with the urge to wrap her fingers around his and never let go.

"I think you're going to be a very good mother, Roslyn. And whatever else you want to be."

His words caused her throat to grow thick with emotion. "You're a morale booster, Chandler."

Thank goodness he hadn't seemed to notice the husky note in her voice. If he ever figured out just how attracted she was to him, he'd probably run for the hills and stay there until she left Three Rivers.

Chuckling, he joked, "You need to come to the clinic and meet my staff. They all call me a tyrant. An exaggeration, in my opinion. Since I don't ask them to do any more than I do during a fourteen-hour workday."

He was teasing, but she seriously wondered why he didn't cut down his work hours.

He'd said he didn't have time for a family of his own. Yet every time she laid eyes on the man she felt certain he'd been born to love a woman, to nurture a brood of children.

Chandler Hollister doesn't want a family, Roslyn. When are you going to get that through your head? The man is thirty-six years old. There's a reason he's chosen to remain a bachelor for so long. And don't go getting the idea that you could be the woman to change him.

Blocking out the cynical voice in her head, she placed a hand on the side of her belly. The subtle movement beneath her fingers reassured her. It also reminded her that the baby would soon be born. Her entire focus would change to being a mother and providing a safe and loving home for her child. There wouldn't be room in her thoughts for a man. Especially a man who had no romantic interest in her at all. And yet, he continued to live in her mind like a sweet, recurring dream.

"You've gone quiet, Roslyn. Are you okay?"

"I'm perfect."

As long as I'm with you.

She didn't know where that thought had come from, but she had a sneaky suspicion it had come straight from her heart.

Chapter Six

Chandler drove for another three miles before he finally stopped the truck next to a wide, shallow creek lined with willows and salt cedar. Off to their left, about a hundred yards away, a herd of black cattle grazed at tufts of grass growing among the chaparral.

"Would you like to walk with me part of the way to see the cattle?" he asked. "Or would you rather remain here in the truck? The engine is diesel, so it's perfectly safe to leave it idling with the air-conditioner going."

"I'm not that much of a softy." She patted the top of her stomach. "I realize this big tummy makes me look off balance, but I'm pretty sure-footed. I'd like to walk with you."

He grinned. "Great. Just stay put and I'll help you down from the truck."

After he'd carefully helped her to the ground, he opened the tailgate and the two dogs leaped out. Roslyn expected them to take off barking and chasing the cattle, but instead they remained obediently at Chandler's side.

"I'm impressed. The dogs aren't running wild. You must be a good trainer," she told him.

He chuckled. "These two are no-nonsense. But a few others get it in their head that it's more fun to play. The key is patience."

"I'm trying to store up all my patience, so I'll have plenty when the baby arrives."

"Better store more for its teenage years. Mom said she couldn't have made it through those years without Dad to keep us corralled."

But her child wouldn't have a dad. Unless she found a man that she loved with all her heart. Some generous-hearted man who wouldn't mind being a father to another man's child.

After a moment passed and she didn't reply, he said, "I'm sorry, Roslyn. I wasn't thinking—about the dad part. But I have a feeling that you're going to have a husband long before that baby gets to be a teenager."

Only if I met someone like you.

And her chances of meeting and marrying a man like Chandler were about the same as finding the end of a rainbow. That kind of stuff only happened in fairy tales. Not in Roslyn's life.

"I wouldn't count on it. But that's years away. Anything can happen." She looked at him and forced a bright smile on her face. "Right?"

He didn't smile back. Instead, he studied her for a long thoughtful moment before he finally murmured, "Sure. Anything can happen."

They walked on toward the herd of gazing cattle and Roslyn purposely turned her attention to their surroundings. The sunshine was hot on her face and the breeze carried the scents of sage and wildflowers. Small birds fluttered around the Joshua trees, while in the far distance, a copse of pines dotted the slopes of a mountain. Roslyn had never been in a wilderness like this before, with nothing around her but rugged land, cattle and wildlife.

The awed appreciation she was feeling must have shown on her face, because he suddenly asked, "I realize I'm repeating myself, but are you okay, Roslyn? You look a bit dazed."

She cast him a quick, reassuring smile. "Sorry, Chandler. I guess I've been staring with my mouth open, haven't I? This land is so beautiful. Everything about it intrigues me. I could probably ask you a thousand questions."

A faint smile tilted his lips. "A thousand questions, huh? Well, ask away. I might be able to answer a few."

"Well, for starters, I'm curious about how many herds of cattle there are on Three Rivers?"

"I can't give you an exact number. The count changes. But it usually ranges around twenty separate herds." He gestured toward the cattle. "This one is number eleven. And the next one we need to look at is number twelve. 'Course, that's not all the cattle we own. We have about three or four more thousand head on our grazing land up by Prescott. And a thousand or so down at Red Bluff. What's the next question?"

"The water. I noticed a creek runs through this little valley. Does it supply enough water during the dry seasons for the cattle to drink?"

"No. This is one of three creeks on the ranch. This one and another a couple of miles from here dry up completely. The other keeps a bit of water in certain places. But we have deep water wells with pumps and other irrigation methods to handle the ranch's needs."

She digested that information, then said, "So there actually are three rivers on the ranch. I figured the ranch's name was just something someone made up."

He shook his head. "My great-great-great-grandfather named the ranch for the three small rivers that converge on our property."

"Gosh, that many 'greats' meant he came to this land a long time ago," she said. "I can't imagine how wild and uninhabited this area must've been back then."

"The first Hollisters came here in 1845. At that time, Edmond and Helena were newlyweds. She was very young—sixteen, I think. He was about ten years older. Mom has a couple of old tintypes of them on their wedding day. I'll show them to you sometime."

"I'd like that," she said, while thinking how very rooted Chandler must feel. He knew why the older generations of Hollisters had come here, why they had stayed and why they would always remain on this spot of ground. How would it feel to have that sort of solid foundation beneath her feet? She could only wonder. She knew very little about her ancestors and those she knew about had been scattered.

"Since there are still Hollisters here on the ranch, I'm assuming Edmond and Helena had children."

"Two boys and a girl," he replied. "My brother Joseph is named after their first son. The girl died as a child from dysentery."

"How sad. I'm sure in those days a medical doctor would've been a long distance away."

"Yes. And medicine wasn't always that helpful."

By now the cattle were less than twenty yards away. Some had lifted their heads and were curiously watching their approach.

Chandler placed a hand on Roslyn's shoulder to stop her forward progress. "This is as close as I want you to get, Roslyn. The cattle are gentle, but sometimes the new mothers can be overly protective. If one charged and hurt you or the baby, I'd never forgive myself." He pointed to their right, where a pair of Joshua trees grew close together. "You might stand over there in the shade. If anything runs in your direction get behind the trees."

"Don't worry. I will."

He walked on into the herd of cattle and Roslyn made her way over to the Joshua trees. From there, she watched as he moved from one calf to the next, searching for signs of scours. Oddly enough, the animals seemed to trust him and several times he managed to get his hands on the calves for a closer examination.

After about ten minutes, she saw him draw a cell phone from his shirt pocket and make a call. Once he'd ended the conversation, he walked over to where she was waiting. He didn't appear overly concerned, but she was learning he was a cool, laid-back type of guy. She'd heard Holt say Chandler was more like their late father than any of the brothers. Perhaps he got his easygoing manner from Joel, along with his striking looks.

"Did some of the cows have pink eye?" she asked.

"A few. I've made a call for some of the hands to bring a trailer out here. I want the calves and their mothers hauled back to the barns at the ranch yard. The cows need to be treated with medications. The calves look okay, but for obvious reasons they need to stay with their mothers."

"Will the cows eyes get well?" she asked.

He nodded. "Yes. Thankfully, the hands spotted the problem early. Blake will appoint two or three men to care for them for the next few days. Don't worry. They'll be fine."

"So what do we do now? Go look at the next herd?"

"Not yet." He wrapped his hand around her arm.

"We'll have to wait here until the cowboys arrive so I can show them which calves need to be loaded. I'm sorry, Roslyn. Looks like it's going to be a long while before we head back to the ranch."

"Don't apologize," she told him. "I'm enjoying every minute of this."

His blue eyes swept over her face and Roslyn got the faint impression he was glad she'd come along. "Okay. Let's walk down to the creek and sit in the shade. Or would you rather wait in the truck?"

"I'm all for the creek," she told him happily. "Just lead the way."

Chandler didn't know what had possessed him to invite Roslyn to join him on this working trek. This wasn't any place for a pregnant woman, who wasn't used to the outdoors. Moreover, spending time with her wasn't really a wise thing to do. For the most part, he didn't want her getting the wrong idea about his motives. She might get to thinking he was in the market for romance, or even worse, for a ready-made family.

But she was just so damn pretty and being with her made him feel young and full of energy. He supposed his brothers, especially Holt, would consider him crazy for being attracted to a pregnant woman. After all, Chandler could easily find himself a date, if he wanted one. There were plenty of women around who were more than willing to go out with him. Some had even gone so far as to call and invite him for a night on the town. But none of those women came close to piquing his interest. And he especially didn't want to waste what little spare time he had being bored by a female whose favorite subject was herself.

Beneath the shade of a gnarled mesquite tree, Chandler sat on a fallen log and allowed his gaze to follow Roslyn's graceful movements as she walked along the creek bank. A pair of butterflies hovering near a branch of blooming salt cedar had presently caught her attention and as he studied her from afar, he decided that being a city girl hadn't stopped her from taking to life here on Three Rivers. It was a fact that surprised him greatly. Although, a part of him wondered if the novelty would soon wear off. The same way it had quickly worn off with Vivian's ex-husband. The ink had hardly dried on his sister's marriage license before Garth had grown bored with living twenty miles from town. A small town at that.

Years had passed before Vivian had finally put their divorce behind her and found the love of her life in Sawyer Whitehorse. His sister was incredibly happy now, but Chandler hadn't forgotten the heartache she'd gone through before she'd met Sawyer. And he sure as hell didn't want to take a chance on the same thing happening to him. And yet there were times he felt very lonely. Times he wished for a woman who would love him and whom he could love in return. A woman he could build a life with and grow old with.

"You're welcome to come share my seat," he called to Roslyn. "You're probably getting tired."

She turned from the water's edge and walked over to where he was sitting. "I'm not really tired, but if it will make you feel better I'll sit," she said.

She eased down next to him and Chandler was suddenly overcome with her nearness and the soft feelings she evoked in him. She smelled of lily of the valley and her skin held an inner glow, as if she'd been sprinkled with stardust. The night at the clinic when she'd fainted, he'd touched her face and wrapped his hand around her tiny wrist. Beneath his fingertips, she'd felt as delicate and smooth as the dewy petal of a flower. Days had passed since that night, yet he'd not forgotten how it had felt to touch her, to cradle her in his arms.

"It'll take a while for the men to get out here with the trailer and then a few more minutes to tag the right cow-calf pairs. If I take you back to the ranch in an exhausted condition, Mom and Reeva will skin my hide."

She laughed lightly and the sound made him smile along with her. It was good to hear her laugh. After all she'd apparently gone through with her father and the broken engagement, he figured she deserved to be happy. He wanted her to be happy.

"Don't worry. I won't cause you to get skinned," she said, then glanced wondrously around her. "There's so much here to look at and experience. I'm never going to forget this place. Thank you for bringing me with you today."

As he watched the wind play with the brown hair lying against her neck, he wondered what she would think if he scooted closer and nuzzled his nose against her cheek. How would she respond if he touched his lips to her lips?

He couldn't allow himself to wonder about such things, he scolded himself. Sure, she'd be here for the next few weeks, but after that she'd be saying goodbye. Kissing her would be all wrong. And yet the urge had been eating at him from the first moment she'd given him one of those sweet smiles.

"Thank you for joining me, Roslyn," he said, while wondering if his voice sounded as strained to her as it did to him. "Cows aren't as good company as you are."

Laughing softly, she turned to look at him and as soon as their gazes met, her laughter sobered. Something warm and smoky filtered into her brown eyes and all of a sudden Chandler was having trouble breathing.

"I—I'm glad to know I provide a bit more companionship than a cow," she murmured.

Before he realized what he was doing, his hand was sliding gently up and down her arm. Surprise flickered across her face, but to his relief she didn't pull away.

"You're very beautiful, Roslyn. I'm sure that's a tired old line you've heard over and over. But that's the way I see you."

She swallowed and he wondered if being near him was affecting her as much as touching her was rattling his senses.

"I'm not beautiful," she protested. "And other than Erich, I've not spent much time in a man's company."

"Why not? And don't tell me the guys back in Fort Worth treated you like a wallflower. I'd never believe it."

She looked out at the shallow water moving sluggishly over the rocky riverbed and Chandler could plainly see sadness etched upon her features. He didn't like seeing it. Didn't like the idea that she'd ever suffered a moment of sorrow.

"Oh, I was asked out often enough. But I usually turned down the offers. I spent most of my teenaged years at home with my mother. You see, all through my high school years she was very sick and I didn't want to leave her alone. Dad hired a private nurse to care for her. But that wasn't the same as having her daughter with her."

"What about your father? Surely he was with his wife."

Her grunt was a mocking sound. "Only when it suited him. And that wasn't often. Don't misunderstand me, Dad always provided lavishly for us. But not with his time or his affections. I guess that's why my mother and I clung to each other. I could see I was losing her and she was basically the only family I had. I realized every minute I spent with her would soon end. So I…"

Her last words trailed off on a hopeless note and he finished the sentence for her. "You neglected yourself in the process."

A faint frown on her face, she looked at him. "I wouldn't call it neglected. I just didn't do the things that my friends were doing at the time. Dances, ballgames, dates—I wasn't much interested. By the time I graduated high school, Mom had grown much worse. I didn't want to go to college, but she insisted. She wanted my life to be normal even though hers wasn't."

"That's because she loved you," he said softly.

She smiled at him, but Chandler was focused more on the bright tears in her eyes.

"How did you know I needed to hear that?" she asked softly.

"Maybe because being a vet isn't always easy. Or maybe because my dad died and I don't really know why. We may never know."

She turned slightly toward him and then her hand reached out and touched the side of his face. The tender contact caused his insides to melt like candy on his tongue.

"Chandler, I—I've never met anyone like you. You make me feel like I'm worth something. You make me feel wanted. And that means more to me than you'll ever know."

Her words should've set off alarm bells in his head. Instead, his heart gathered them up like a starving man at the dinner table.

Leaning toward her, his eyes delved into hers. "I've never met anyone like you, Roslyn. And I'm glad you stopped at the clinic. Glad our paths met that night."

"Really?"

Doubt put a waver in her voice, but Chandler's was

strong and steady as he answered. "Yes. Really. Otherwise, I'd never know what it was like to know you—to do this."

Her eyebrows lifted slightly. "This?"

All finished with thinking, Chandler cupped a hand against the back of her head and drew his face close to hers.

"Chandler, what are you…doing? Thinking…?"

As she whispered the question, her warm breath fanned his lips. The sensation was totally erotic and whetted his appetite to kiss her even more.

"I'm not thinking," he admitted, desire turning his voice gruff. "I'm hoping…that you want to kiss me as much as I want to kiss you."

"I do. Oh, yes, Chandler, I do."

Her response barely had time to register in his brain before she took the initiative and touched her lips to his.

Soft. Incredibly soft. Like the wisps of a cloud brushing against his face. She kissed each corner of his lips, then moved to a nearby dimple. Chandler exhaled a shaky breath, while his fingers tangled around her silky hair.

She whispered his name again and then her lips were back on his, open, fierce and hungry. Giving him exactly what he wanted and more.

Groaning with pleasure, Chandler's arms instantly wrapped around her shoulders and drew her upper body close to his. She moaned in response and, not caring about the consequences, he deepened the kiss until their surroundings faded to little more than flashes of sky and ground.

He hardly noticed the insistent buzzing in his shirt pocket and even when he did recognize the sound as his phone, he chose to ignore it.

But Roslyn didn't. She pulled back and sucked in a shaky breath. "You should probably answer that," she said, her gaze purposely avoiding his. “It might be an emergency.”

Her raspy voice sounded as though she’d just woken from a deep sleep, making him wonder if she’d been just as lost in their kiss as he’d been.

Hell, Chandler, even if she had been turned on by you, that didn’t mean anything. Except that she wasn’t immune to physical pleasure. Don’t be a fool and start thinking the kiss had been important to her. You’ve gone down that road before and it’s a road to nowhere. Just remember that.

Shoving out a long breath, he did his best to ignore the jaded voice in his head. “Yeah. I’ll see who it is,” he muttered. “Could be the hands trying to locate which range we’re on.”

Roslyn rose from the log and while she ambled over to a shady portion at the water’s edge, Chandler pulled the cell phone from his pocket. Seeing the call had originated from the clinic, he punched the call-back button and Cybil answered before the first ring ended. She immediately apologized for interrupting him, then hurriedly went on to explain a situation with two kittens suffering from coccidia.

Chandler patiently instructed, “Yes, if the test came back showing coccidia parasites they’ll need to be dosed immediately. With the same medication we use for the swine and poultry. Just weigh each kitten carefully. If they’re alert and willing to drink, don’t bother with drips. The owner can take them back home. If they’re weak and listless better hold them over and hydrate them. Ten days of medication and soft food. Got it?”

After Cybil had assured him she had all the instructions she needed, Chandler ended the call and walked over to stand next to Roslyn. She didn’t bother to look at him. Instead she stared straight ahead as though she'd decided the two of them had connected enough for one day.

"Sorry for the interruption, Roslyn. My assistant back at the clinic is trying to deal with sick kittens without my help. Intestinal issues. Must be the day for such things," he said wryly.

"Must be," she quietly replied.

He touched a hand to her shoulder and she glanced up at him. As her brown eyes scanned his face, he could see they were shadowed with confusion and doubts. Damn it! He'd not meant to cause her any anguish or uncertainty. He'd simply wanted to be close to her. He still wanted it.

"I hope you're not sorry about that kiss, Roslyn. I don't want you to…regret what just happened with us."

A lost, lonely sigh slipped past her lips and Chandler desperately wanted to pull her into his arms. He wanted to reassure her that she could trust him to never hurt her. But could he really make her such a promise, when he had no idea what she might eventually ask from him?

"I don't regret it," she said quietly. "I'm just a little embarrassed because— Oh, I don't know why I—"

When she didn't continue, he gently squared her shoulders so that she was facing him. "I don't know why you'd be embarrassed, Roslyn. Because it was nice. Very nice."

She closed her eyes and swallowed and for a moment Chandler thought she was about to cry. And he didn't know what he'd do if a tear did roll down her cheek. Hate himself for the rest of his life, he supposed.

Her eyes opened and he could see a look of wonder swimming in the brown depths. "But I kissed you like… well, you're probably thinking I'm some sort of hussy or something. That it's no wonder I'm pregnant out of wedlock."

If she hadn't look so remorseful he would've laughed

out loud. "Roslyn, you're thinking is so off the mark it's funny. But I'm not going to laugh. Because I can see that you're serious and…oh, honey, you are so—" He cupped his hand to the side of her face and in that moment it felt as though his heart was about to burst with some strange, new emotion he'd never felt before. "You're precious, Roslyn. You could never be a hussy."

"So you say. But I'm not going to pretend, Chandler. When I'm with you I'm really not myself." She frowned. "I'm beginning to wonder if these last days of my pregnancy are doing something to my senses."

Smiling, he stroked the tip of his forefinger along the shell-pink color splashed across her cheekbone. "What's my excuse? I'm the one who instigated the whole thing."

"You're a man. You don't need a reason to kiss a woman. Do you?"

Her question caused the smile on his face to linger. "I always thought a reason was necessary. But in your case, just looking at you gives me a good enough reason."

Her nostrils flared as she drew in a deep breath and then she was pulling away and turning her back to him. "I'm eight months pregnant in case you haven't noticed."

"I've noticed. A lot." He stepped around to the front of her and laid a hand on the side of her belly. "You know, in my line of work I see pregnancy just about every day. Yes, I'm talking about animals now. But animal or human, it's a wondrous and beautiful thing. If you're thinking your thick waistline makes you any less desirable than the next woman, your thinking is all wrong."

Her eyes misted over and Chandler suddenly realized that she was far more to him than a pretty face with soft, kissable lips. But he could hardly admit the fact to himself, much less to her.

"Chandler, I'm only going to be here for a few weeks. I don't think it would be wise to let myself kiss you again."

Even though he understood that she was probably being practical and smart, her words left him flat. And somewhat surprised. Especially after the passionate way she'd responded to his kiss. But perhaps she was right about this last stage of her pregnancy affecting her senses. Under other circumstances she might not have been interested in kissing him in any form or fashion.

After all, she was eleven years younger. He probably came across as an old man to her. Not a guy she'd want to start a relationship with.

Relationship. Was that what he wanted with Roslyn? Something more than a few dates? Something that wouldn't end with a kiss on the cheek and a relieved goodbye?

The questions were bantering around in his brain when the movement of the baby rippled beneath his hand. The sensation waylaid his revolving thoughts and he looked at her with new appreciation.

"The baby must be taking dance lessons. Right now I think she's doing a tap number."

She smiled. "I'm beginning to think my child is going to be a dancer or some sort of athlete."

The night she'd fainted at the clinic and he'd listened to the baby's heartbeat, he'd been in doctor mode. Only the health of the child had been in his thoughts. But everything was different now. Roslyn was swiftly becoming a part of his life, along with the baby. He didn't know whether that was a good or bad thing. Either way, he couldn't seem to stop his feelings from escalating.

He smiled back at her. "Or a rancher, schoolteacher, doctor—anything he or she wants to be," he suggested.

She pressed a hand over his and the contact reminded

him that the baby had veered their conversation on a different path. With the ranch hands likely to arrive any moment, he wanted to get back to what had just happened between them.

"About the kiss, Roslyn. I think we were both enjoying it. And I don't think it would be unwise for me to kiss you again. Or for you to kiss me. If that's what we both wanted," he added slyly.

For a moment she looked ready to argue the point, but then her lips pressed together and created an impish dimple in her left cheek. "Chandler, I'm beginning to think your nickname should be Naughty Doc rather than just Doc."

In the time it took blink his eyes, she'd chosen to make light of the whole thing. Which was probably best for both of them, Chandler decided. He shouldn't want to make an issue over one little kiss. Trouble was for Chandler, it had been far more than just one little kiss.

He coughed up a chuckle and hoped it sounded authentic. Behind them, the rattle of a fast-approaching stock trailer signaled the arrival of the ranch hands.

"The cowboys are here," she said, stating the obvious.

"Yeah. I'd better get over to the herd."

"I'll wait here," she informed him. "I don't want to get in the way and be a nuisance."

A nuisance? Never, he thought, as he walked briskly out to join the men. But she was definitely a lovely temptation. One that he damn well needed to resist. Otherwise, when she left Three Rivers, she was liable to take his heart with her.

Chapter Seven

Two days later, Chandler showed up halfway through the evening meal. As he took a seat next to Roslyn, she noticed his damp black hair had been combed back from his face and the tails of a white shirt tucked haphazardly into his jeans. He looked even more fatigued than usual and Roslyn was suddenly overwhelmed with the urge to wrap her arms around him.

"Sorry, everyone, for being late," he apologized. "Things got hectic at the clinic."

Blake passed a platter of what was left of the fried chicken down the table to Chandler. "Things are *always* hectic at the clinic," Blake said with an edge of impatience. "I don't know when you're going to break down and hire more help. Specifically another vet to handle the patients you don't have time for."

Chandler forked two pieces of chicken onto his plate, then reached for a bowl of mashed potatoes. "I *specifi-*

cally don't want another vet," he replied to his brother's comment. "I might not like the way he does things. And I sure as hell don't want the clinic's reputation ruined by an outside quack."

"Wow, Chandler, who put a burr under your saddle?" Holt asked from his seat across the table.

Roslyn had been wondering the same thing. She'd never seen Chandler show this much frustration before.

"You two, leave your brother alone," Maureen said to Blake and Holt. "Can't you see he's stressed?"

Holt snickered. "Stressed. Chandler needs to try climbing on a bunch of two-year-olds and he'll learn what stress really is. That's after his ass hits the ground a few times."

Roslyn watched a muscle jump in Chandler's jaw, but he refrained from making a retort.

Down the table, Maureen glared at her younger son, while Blake shook his head. "Ease up, Holt. You know good and well that our brother puts in far too many hours working."

"I don't want anyone's sympathy." Chandler's voice was gruff, and his eyebrows pulled together in a scowl. "What I need is more help at the clinic. And not another vet," he said to Blake. "Cybil's sister had some sort of accident and hurt her back. The past few days she's been taking off to help care for her sister's kids."

Holt slapped a hand on the tabletop. "I got it, brother! Why don't you let Roslyn help you out? I'm sure she'd love dealing with the small animals."

"That's a wonderful idea, Holt," Maureen said, then directed an encouraging smile at Roslyn. "What do you say, Ros? Have you ever spent any time at an animal clinic?"

Roslyn wondered how the conversation had moved so

quickly to include her. “Um, no. I haven’t,” she answered Maureen. “Other than recuperating in Chandler’s office the night I fainted. But I’d be willing to learn.”

Judging from the glower on Chandler’s face, he wanted miles and miles separating her from his animal clinic.

He slanted a rueful glance at her. “I don’t think that would be wise, Roslyn. You’d have to be on your feet. And you’d have to avoid the cat litter. And—”

“Chandler, quit being a stuffed shirt,” Maureen interrupted. “Roslyn is young and healthy. Lots of women work on their feet right up until they give birth. Why, when I was pregnant with you kids I was riding up until my seventh month and helping in the branding pen up until my due date. Roslyn is a woman who’s going to have a baby. Not a piece of porcelain you have to keep safely on a shelf.”

“Maureen is right,” Roslyn told him. “I’m not a weakling. In fact, the exercise will be good for me. And helping out at the clinic would make me feel productive instead of like a sponge.”

Unconvinced, he said, “You don’t know the first thing about animals.”

“Well, I can always fetch things for you and clean up,” she argued. “That should help a little. And I can learn the rest as I go.”

“Sounds good to me,” Holt said with a grin, then asked shrewdly, “Or are you afraid the place will run over with guys wanting to get a look at your pretty assistant?”

“Blake, would you please stuff a chicken leg in Holt’s mouth?” Maureen said. “Anything to shut him up.”

Holt laughed. “Oh, Mom, you know I’m only teasing Chandler. He’d think I was sick if I didn’t give him a hard time.”

Maureen drained her wineglass, then reached for the

tall, dark bottle sitting near her elbow. Roslyn had never seen the woman refill her glass at dinner, but maybe the trip she'd made to Phoenix this morning had made the day extra taxing for her.

"Yes, you're always teasing, Holt. But instead of telling Chandler what he *ought* to be doing, why don't you tell us what you *have* been doing—with the horses. I had a long conversation today with the foreman of the Tumbleweed Ranch in Nevada. They're wanting twenty head of our mares and ten yearlings."

"Twenty head of mares?" Holt guffawed. "Over my dead body. They're the lifeblood of our remuda. And we've never sold a yearling off this ranch before. Each one has a chance to prove himself worthy of a lifetime home here on Three Rivers. Surely you set him straight on all of that, didn't you?"

From the corner of her eye, Roslyn noticed Chandler was carefully watching his mother's reaction.

"No. I told him we might be able to come up with half that number," Maureen quipped, then took another long sip of wine. "But I did explain that he'd need to talk with you and Blake before a deal could be made."

Holt's mouth dropped open and for a split second Roslyn thought the man was going to curse a blue streak in front of his mother and everyone else. But just as quickly, his jaw snapped shut and he directed a dark stare at Blake.

Blake slanted their mother an annoyed look, before turning his gaze back to his younger brother. "Don't worry, Holt. I'll give the foreman a call and explain to him that our number of broodmares is exactly where we want it to be. And the yearlings are off-limits."

After Blake's words trailed away, no one else made any kind of remark about the horses. And for the first time since Roslyn had come to the ranch, the atmosphere around the Hollister dinner table felt strained.

The remainder of the meal passed in silence and afterward, Roslyn chose to skip dessert in the den. Instead, she carried a cup of coffee to the front porch, where she could watch the last streaks of red-gold sunlight sink below a row of desert hills.

"Care if I join you?"

Roslyn glanced around to see Chandler stepping onto the porch and closing the door behind him.

"You're very welcome to join me," she told him. "It's a beautiful evening out here."

He walked over to where she stood resting a shoulder against one of the porch post.

"And as awkward as hell inside," he added wryly. "Sorry about all that at the dinner table, Roslyn. I hope you know it's nothing about you. Sometimes we get on each other's nerves."

She turned so that she was facing him. "From what I've gathered since I've been here, Holt is very particular about the horses. I got the impression he was more than a little vexed with your mother when she mentioned selling a few."

He let out a heavy sigh. "Long before Dad died, he appointed Holt manager of the horse division. And rightly so. He knows equines inside and out. And to tell you the truth, he can probably doctor them as good, or better than I can. He loves each and every baby he raises like his own child, and he only sells the ones that end up unable to handle the rigors of ranch work. Holt always has the final say so over the horses. That's why…it seemed a little peculiar to us brothers that Mom didn't set the Nevada rancher straight, right off. And for her to imply we might sell ten mares and five yearlings—it's worrisome, Roslyn. She's not herself."

Could be he was also thinking his mother had been amiss when she'd agreed with the suggestion of Roslyn working at the clinic. She hoped not. The idea of working with Chandler and his staff was very appealing. True, it would allow her to spend more time in his company, but it would also give her a real purpose until the baby arrived.

She said, "Maureen was gone to Phoenix for most of the day today—to a cattle-buyers meeting. I'm sure she's tired."

He frowned. "Hmm. She's gone to Phoenix several times in the past few months. I wasn't aware she was going again today."

"I heard her telling Reeva that she'd decided at the last minute to go." She darted a glance at him. "And now you're going to think I go around the house eavesdropping on conversations."

Smiling wanly, he touched a forefinger to the tip of her nose. "Your nose is too little to make you a busybody. But let's forget about Mom for now. We need to discuss this matter about you and the clinic. Let's go sit," he suggested.

With his hand against the small of her back, he guided her over to a wicker love seat padded with striped cushions. The touch of his hand was warm and instantly reminded her of the kiss they'd shared out on the range.

That kiss. She'd never experienced anything like it before. Even now, the memory of the embrace heated her cheeks and twisted knots in the pit of her stomach. Kissing Chandler had been like downing a shot of straight whiskey—wickedly hot and instantly intoxicating. These past couple of days, she'd been desperately trying to get the whole incident out of her mind. But rather than forgetting, her thoughts had been stuck on *that kiss*. And him.

"Look, Chandler, I'm sorry your mother and brother put you on the spot about me working at the clinic. If you're afraid I'll be in the way, I'll understand."

"I never said I thought you'd be in the way."

She shook her head. "You didn't have to. I could see misgivings on your face. But that's okay. You and your family have already done so much for me. You hardly need to give me a job."

He reached for her hand and she gladly allowed him to fold her fingers inside his big warm palm.

"My reservations have nothing to do with you getting underfoot. If that was the case I would've fired Trey a year ago. I'm more concerned about your health and the baby's."

"Well, if I start getting weary, I can always sit down and put up my feet. You see, I know the boss," she added impishly. "He won't mind."

His eyes twinkled. "I see—you're already expecting favoritism."

She chuckled. "Just a little."

"Well, you'd have to drive yourself back and forth to the clinic. Riding with me is out of the question. Some days I might be leaving at four thirty in the morning and not returning until midnight."

"That's no problem. If the ranch has an extra vehicle I can use, I know how to drive," she reasoned.

He squeezed her fingers. "Just the drive here and back might be tiring for you."

"Oh, Chandler, I'm not that fragile. Really. And it would make me feel good to be able to do something for you—to take some of the work off your shoulders."

As he studied her face, she couldn't help notice how

the last rays of sunlight were touching his face, illuminating the black whiskers that had emerged above his dark skin. Just thinking about touching her lips to his jaw and experiencing the raspy sensation against the tip of her tongue was enough to send a shiver down her spine.

"You mean that, don't you?"

Her gaze met his and she wondered if he could see the feelings that were billowing up inside of her, making her ache to touch him.

"I do," she said simply.

His eyes remained connected to hers for another long moment before he finally looked away. "I'm not sure it's the right thing to do. But I can see the whole thing is important to you."

"It's very important, Chandler. When I leave here with my baby I'm eventually going to have to find a job. I want to be able to tell an employer that I've worked for a few days in my life, at least. But more than that, I need to prove to myself that I can contribute."

"You've already told me that you did volunteer work back in Fort Worth. Obviously you can contribute to a cause."

"That's true," she admitted. "And my work there was appreciated. But it's not the same as punching a time clock."

Chandler laughed. "Thankfully my staff doesn't punch a time clock. Otherwise, I'd have to pay them for so much overtime, I'd go broke."

Roslyn chuckled along with him. "Well, Doc, you wouldn't have to worry about paying me anything. I'd be an intern."

His expression sobered and Roslyn's breath caught in her throat as his thumb gently stroked the back of her hand.

"No pay. No job."

"Oh, but—" She started to argue and then her eyes widened with sudden dawning. "Are you saying that you're going to give me a try at the clinic?"

He shrugged as a wry smile tilted one corner of his lips. "Against my better judgment. But the minute it becomes too much for you to handle, that's it."

With a little cry of delight, she flung her arms around his neck and smacked a kiss on his cheek. "Thank you, Chandler. Thank you!"

"You're very welcome," he murmured.

For a moment, his hand came up to mesh in her hair and while she savored the feel of his fingers against her scalp, she allowed her cheek to rest against his and her nostrils to breathe in the masculine scent of his hair and skin.

He was rough and rugged and all hard muscle. And she could have stayed like that forever, close to him, touching him. But the door to the house opened and she pulled back before anyone could spot the embrace.

"Well, I wondered where you two had gone."

Holt walked over and sank into a chair sitting at an angle to Chandler's side of the love seat. He was carrying a squatty glass partially filled with ice and a dark liquid that Roslyn assumed was whiskey and cola.

"I figured you were in the den with your feet up. Enjoying coffee and pie," Chandler said to him.

"It's too damn quiet in the den," he remarked. "It's like a tomb in there. And tonight I need something a heck of a lot stronger than coffee."

"Katherine never showed up with Andy and Abby, or Nick?" Chandler asked. "The twins would supply plenty of noise."

Holt shook his head. "According to Blake, Nick has

gone over to the reservation to stay the night with Hannah. And the twins are fussy from teething and Katherine is keeping them upstairs this evening so their crying won't get on everyone's nerves."

"Aww, I should go help her," Roslyn said. "She probably hasn't had a chance to eat dinner."

"Blake is helping her," Holt informed her. "Please don't leave me out here alone with only my hairy-legged brother for company. I've had a hell of a day. And you're a much prettier diversion than he is."

Chandler cocked an eyebrow at him. "What's been happening today? Been breaking colts?"

"Only this morning. The afternoon I spent with Joe. You know how he and Blake go out every week searching for clues. Well, Blake had a bunch of banking business to deal with today and couldn't go. So that left me to go with Joe—this time on horseback. I was beginning to think it was going to take an earthquake to get Joe headed back to the ranch. We were out there for hours."

Roslyn could see Chandler's interest was suddenly piqued. He leaned slightly toward his brother. "Find anything more than rock and sagebrush?"

Snorting, he answered, "Two sidewinders and a Gila monster. One of the sidewinders nearly got my hand. I was moving a rock and didn't see it."

"Nothing pertaining to Dad?" Chandler persisted.

Holt nodded. "That's why I came out here to talk to you. I didn't want to mention any of this in front of Mom. God knows she's not been herself here lately. And you know how she's gotten about Dad's death. She doesn't want us digging, or looking, or even talking about any of it."

Chandler's sigh was burdened with worry. "Yeah. I know. But that doesn't mean we have to stop searching for answers. That's our right. He was our father. If we ever do get enough to put a theory together, then we can tell her."

"That's the way Joe and Blake feel about it, too." He wiped a hand over his face, then dug into the front pocket of his jeans. "We found two things today. That's why Joe didn't want to quit. He was like a bloodhound that had picked up the scent of the trail."

He handed Chandler the two items. "Do those look familiar?"

Chandler leaned back in the love seat and closely examined the small objects in the palm of his hand. One was a triangle of tattered fabric, the other an intricately carved piece of silver shaped like the end of a leather belt.

Chandler's eyes widened perceptively. "Why, this is a piece of Dad's shirt! The blue-and-gray plaid he had on the day he died. And this belt tip—there's no doubt it was his! That's his initials on the back. Didn't Blake give that to him for a birthday gift?"

Holt nodded soberly. "We found them not far from water well number nine."

Shaking his head with disbelief, Chandler said, "But we've gone over and over that area. How did you happen to stumble across these?"

Holt took a long swig of his drink and as Roslyn's gaze bounced between the two men, it was very clear that this was a significant finding. Not that she knew any particulars about their father's death. Except that they'd found Joel dangling from beneath his horse. His boot had hung in the stirrup and he'd been lugged over the ground for a long distance.

"You remember the arroyo where we found Dad's spur rowel?" Holt asked.

Chandler nodded as he tested the weave of the fabric

between his thumb and forefinger. The colors were very faded and the edges jagged and frayed. Roslyn could only wonder what he was thinking and feeling. Even to this day, it hurt her deeply to look at her mother's clothing and personal items, which were still stored away in her bedroom. A room that, to Roslyn, seemed like a prison cell. For so many reasons.

"That was about two years ago." Chandler leveled a skeptical look at Holt. "Don't tell me these things were near it!"

"Not there. About a quarter mile north is a narrow gulch that runs for about two hundred yards. For some reason Joe got the hunch that we ought to look in it. He found the belt tip at the bottom of the wash. I found the piece of fabric hung on a juniper root about midway up the bank."

Chandler's head swung back and forth as though he was having trouble digesting Holt's news. "What does Joe think now?"

"We all thought that whatever happened with Dad initially took place in the first gulch by the water well, right?"

Chandler said, "It's a logical assumption since that's where his spur rowel was found. But these things you've found today puts a hole in that theory."

"After today, Joe seems to believe the fight, or ambush, or whatever the hell occurred, started in the gulch north of there. Afterward, Major Bob took off running in the direction of home. That would have most likely carried the horse, with Dad dragging from the stirrup, into the gulch where the spur rowel was dislodged."

The horrible image caused Roslyn to outwardly shiver and Chandler immediately wrapped his arm protectively around her shoulders. "You're getting cold, Roslyn. We should go in."

"No. I'm not cold. I'm just thinking—" She hesitated, unsure of how to convey her thoughts on the matter. "Well, it's none of my business, but from a woman's viewpoint, I can understand why Maureen wants to put Joel's death behind her. I'm sure each time the subject is brought up, a piece of her heart is torn out."

Holt said, "That's why she's not going to see these things. I'm going to let Joe keep them over at the Bar X. That way there won't be any chance of her stumbling across them."

Chandler nodded, then asked his brother, "Did you know Mom had gone to Phoenix today?"

"Not until Reeva told me and Joe before we left the ranch right after lunch. Why?"

"Because I think she's doing more than going to a cattleman's meeting."

Holt made a cynical grunt. "Hell, Chandler, of course she's doing more than that. You think she'd go to Phoenix without doing some shopping for her grandkids?"

Chandler cast a wry glance at Roslyn, then turned his attention back to Holt. "She probably is doing a bit of shopping. But I also think she might be seeing Uncle Gil."

"Who's Uncle Gil?" Roslyn asked, then, realizing how she sounded, quickly apologized. "Forgive me, you two. This is none of my business. In fact, I really should go inside and let you two discuss your family in private."

Chandler kept his arm firmly around her shoulders. "Sit still."

"Yeah, sit still, Roslyn," Holt added. "You're living here with us and that makes you close to being family."

"And we know you're not going to repeat any of this," Chandler added.

"Of course not. To tell you the truth, I've been all ears because I—I'm so fond of Maureen. She's been so good to me and she deserves to be happy. But tonight at dinner she seemed far from it."

Chandler's expression softened as he looked at Roslyn. "That's why I was harping on the trip to Phoenix. There's some connection there."

"You mentioned Uncle Gil," Holt prodded. "Why? Mom visits him from time to time when she goes to Phoenix. That's no secret."

Chandler explained to Roslyn. "Uncle Gil is our father's brother. He's worked for the city police department for many years. He's an investigator now."

"Oh." She thought about this for a moment. "Then you're thinking she's asked him to do some sort of investigating? About your father?"

"That's possible," Holt said.

Chandler shook his head. "No. I'm thinking she's seeing him—like in an emotionally dependent way."

Holt swore beneath his breath. Not at Chandler, but at the whole idea about their mother. "Have you gone daffy, brother? Mom was crazy about Dad. She worshipped the ground he walked on."

"That's exactly why I'm thinking this," Chandler told him. "She needs someone outside of us kids to lean on—to share her feelings with. Gil knows Mom well and he's like Dad in so many ways. Would it be that crazy for her to feel drawn to the man?"

Holt belted back the last of his drink. "Hell, Chandler, nothing surprises me anymore. I just wish Viv hadn't moved so far away. I miss her so much."

Chandler was about to make some sort of reply when the buzzing of a phone sounded.

Holt looked around. "Is that someone's phone going off?"

"It's yours," Chandler told him. "Mine is in the house on the charger."

Heaving out a weary breath, Holt pulled the phone from his jeans pocket. As soon as he glanced at the face, he rose to his feet. "You two enjoy the rest of your evening. I have to go to the horse barn."

"Need help?" Chandler asked.

"Thanks, brother. Not this time."

Holt didn't bother going back into the house to change clothes or return his whiskey glass. Instead he leaped off the end of the porch and took off in a long stride toward the horse barn.

Chandler watched his brother move off into the rapidly falling darkness. "Holt is overworked," he said. "But he's too stubborn to hire another horse trainer to help him with the load. He doesn't think anyone can handle the horses as well as he does."

"Seems like I've heard that his older brother suffers from the same sort of mind-set," Roslyn said shrewdly.

He cast her a sheepish look, then chuckled. "It's something that runs in our DNA, I guess. Blake had it, too. Until marrying Katherine finally convinced him to hire a secretary."

"I've not met Florence, but I've heard your mother speak highly of her," Roslyn told him. "How does Blake feel about having a secretary?"

"It took him a while to trust Florence with important matters. But he soon learned she's like a drill sergeant—no-nonsense. Now if he needs to be out of the office, he doesn't think twice about leaving her in charge. And he doesn't have to work after dinner to catch up on paperwork."

Roslyn gave him a coy smile. "Instead, he can spend time with his wife and children."

"Point well taken," he said. "But I already have six employees to help me run the clinic. Two work up front to deal with appointments and paperwork. Two more assist me in the treatment rooms and two more help me take care of the large animals outside the clinic."

The night Roslyn had fainted, she recalled meeting Trey, but other than him, she'd not seen any other staff members around the place. She'd guessed he might have two or three employees all together. "Wow! I had no idea. You must be an extremely good veterinarian."

He let out a short laugh. "I don't know about good. But I'm the *only* vet in the area. Otherwise, a person has to drive down toward Phoenix or as far north as Prescott to get an animal treated."

"Now I understand why you have such a heavy workload. And why your family thinks you should hire an associate."

The hand resting against her upper arm moved up and down ever so slightly against her bare skin. Roslyn instinctively wanted to scoot closer to his side and rest her head upon his strong shoulder. She wanted to tell him how much she adored every moment of his company. But would he even care to know her intimate thoughts?

His short laugh had nothing to do with being amused. "My family wants me to work less at the clinic and more here on the ranch. Which I understand. I'm a Hollister. I should be doing my fair share. But I don't want to be restricted to just working here on Three Rivers. Do you know how many suffering animals would go without medical care if I had never opened the clinic?"

"Many, I'm sure," she answered.

"Over the years, the count would be in the hundreds and hundreds. I wouldn't be happy about that."

"No. You wouldn't be happy," she agreed.

A stretch of silence passed and as the baby's movements pushed against her abdomen, she wondered what she was really doing here, living with a family she'd met only two weeks ago. Deluding herself? Dreaming that Chandler might grow some serious feelings toward her and the baby? She was being a fool.

He said, "Now you're sitting there wondering why I don't hire an associate."

"I don't have to wonder. I can see that you're like Holt in that manner. You want things done as you would do them. And I imagine that finding another veterinarian with your dedication would be hard to do."

Appreciation softened his features. "I think you do understand."

More than he'd ever guess, Roslyn thought, glumly. Yes, he was as particular about his animal clinic as Holt was about Three Rivers horseflesh. The two men were proud of their abilities and their reputations. And rightly so. But with Chandler, she got the impression there was another reason altogether why he liked going solo. Working fourteen hours a day gave him a good excuse not to get seriously involved with a woman. Not to tie himself to a marriage and children. Why he wanted to avoid that kind of commitment, she didn't know. Nor should she want to know. But God help her, she did.

"I try," she said wanly, then scooted to the edge of the seat with the intention of rising to her feet. "I think it's time I get back inside. Jazelle went home early, so Reeva might need some help in the kitchen."

Chandler's hand wrapped over her forearm. "Not yet. There's something I want to discuss with you."

Her heart began to tap out an anxious rhythm as she turned her head to look at him. Had he already decided he didn't want her at the clinic? Or did he want to talk about that torrid kiss they'd shared out on the range?

"Okay. About what?"

"Your father."

His blunt answer jolted her and sent her mind spinning with questions. Why should Martin DuBose concern him? Unless…oh, no! Surely he or someone else in the family hadn't gone back on their word and contacted him. If so, she'd have to run again. She'd have to leave Three Rivers Ranch and Chandler behind.

She wasn't ready for that. She wasn't sure she'd ever be ready to tell this man goodbye.

Chapter Eight

A cool chill ran through Roslyn and she wrapped her arms around herself in an attempt to ward off a shiver. “My father? What about him?”

His gaze scanned her face and Roslyn noticed how even in the waning twilight, his blue eyes were vivid and oh, so striking.

“About contacting him and letting him know where you are,” he answered.

She tried not to gasp. Did Chandler honestly believe she ought to contact her father? If he did, it was because he didn’t understand.

“No. I haven’t gotten in touch with him by phone or mail or any other way,” she stiffly. “And it will be a long time before I do.”

Silence followed her sharp reply and then he finally said, “I was just thinking that, well, now that you’ve been here a while and had time to ponder about everything, that you might’ve had a change of heart.”

She was so surprised by his comment that she twisted around on the seat in order to face him head-on. "Are you joking, Chandler? A change of heart? I'm sorry. I know he's my father and I shouldn't have ill feelings toward him, but I—" She shook her head. "I can't deal with him now. He'd be threatening to take my baby, my money, everything I have just to pressure me back under his wing."

"That's hard to believe. Why would he be that callous to his own daughter?"

She let out an unladylike snort. "Because he's a controlling man. Because my being pregnant and single, and now a runaway, has put a blight on his good name. He wants to try to smooth it all over. And having me home would make it appear that all was well within our family. What little is left of it," she added bitterly.

"That kind of thinking went out the door years ago," he argued.

She nodded ruefully. "My father is seventy now. Not that his age is an excuse. But he was raised in a different culture. Where women were expected to remain in the background."

"People can change. And a baby has a way of changing a person," Chandler gently suggested. "Could be that once your father gets a look at his grandchild his whole attitude will soften."

A pang of regret hit Roslyn's chest. "That would be wonderful, Chandler. But I don't much believe in fairy tales anymore. Do you?"

His hand slid up her arm and wrapped over the top of her shoulder. For a moment Roslyn thought he was going to pull her into his arms. Or, at least, that's what every fiber in her body was screaming for him to do. But instead, his fingers began to knead her flesh, which promptly sent rivulets of heat throughout her body.

"No. But you hiding yourself away from your parent isn't good, Roslyn. Not for you or your baby."

"Maybe it isn't," she admitted. "But I'm not ready to risk this freedom I have right now, Chandler."

He gave her a wan smile. "Well, talking about Dad's death a few minutes ago—it made me wish better things for you, Roslyn."

Her heart melting, she leaned forward and touched a hand to the side of his face. "It made me wish better things for both of us," she whispered.

A groan sounded deep in his throat and then his lips were suddenly brushing against her cheek and over her nose. Softly, gently, he continued on a downward path, purposely avoiding her lips. By the time he planted a tiny kiss in the middle of her chin, her breathing had turned into shallow little sups and her heart was beating with slow, anxious thuds.

She sighed as the scent of him filtered into her nostrils and filled her head with erotic desires that no pregnant woman should be feeling. But, oh, she *was* thinking and feeling. And she wanted more from him. So much more.

"I've been thinking about our kiss, Roslyn. A lot."

Our kiss. Yes, it had been a together thing, she thought, with one giving as much as the other. During those moments in his arms she'd never felt so connected to a man or so totally and wonderfully lost in his kiss.

"I would've never guessed it," she murmured.

His chuckle was low and sexy and caused his breath to warm her lips.

"Why? Because I haven't tried to repeat it?"

"Something like that."

"You said it be unwise to kiss me again. Remember?"

Her hands trembled as she placed them upon his chest.

The warmth beneath her palms made her want to push aside his shirt and explore the hard expanse of muscle.

"I remember. But I could've been…wrong."

"You were wrong." His lips lightly grazed hers. "Because something this good has to be right."

Wise or not, by now, Roslyn didn't care. She wanted him. In all the ways a woman could want a man.

With a tiny groan, she leaned into him and curled her arms around his neck. He reacted by fastening his lips over hers in a searching kiss.

Instantly, her senses were plunged into a vortex of pleasure so great that it rendered her helpless. All she could do was hang onto him and hope the kiss never ended.

Unfortunately, Chandler did finally break the contact between them, and as his head pulled away from hers, Roslyn was stunned and embarrassed to feel a mist of tears fill her eyes.

Not wanting him to guess how emotionally shaken the kiss had left her, she quickly rose from the seat and walked to the edge of the porch.

As she stood there, staring out at the night sky, she was forced to link her hands together to still their trembling. Yet nothing could stop the quiver that had started somewhere deep inside her and settled in the middle of her chest.

And she didn't need a doctor to diagnose the cause of her malady. She'd been struck by a massive dose of fear. She was falling for the wrong man. Again.

"Roslyn? Are you angry with me?"

She swallowed and hoped she could speak without sounding like she was choking. "No. Why should I be angry?"

"I'm not sure. Unless you're thinking I'm just being a flirt—playing with you."

Aren't you? She pushed the question off her tongue. Asking it would ruin everything. He'd have to admit that he didn't have serious intentions toward her and that would make it very awkward to work with him at the clinic. No, if she was going to leave Three Rivers with even a shred of pride, she needed to keep the question to herself. And her feelings under wrap.

"Don't worry, Chandler. I'm not thinking that you're getting serious. After all, it was just a little kiss. I'm sure you've had hundreds of them. The majority much nicer than mine." She stepped past him. "If you'll excuse me, I really need to go in now."

Before she was halfway to the door, his hand closed around her upper arm. Her mouth open, she whirled around to confront him, but he didn't give her time to get one word out.

He tugged her into the circle of his arms and plastered a long, searing kiss on her lips.

By the time he lifted his head, she could only stare in total bewilderment at the raw look of desire on his face.

"Even if I'd had a thousand kisses none of them would come close to being as nice as yours."

Too stunned to utter a word, she pulled out of his arms and hurried into the house.

By the middle of the next week, Roslyn felt as though she was a full-fledged employee at Hollister Animal Hospital and she was enjoying every minute she spent there. The four women and two men already on staff had welcomed her warmly and made her feel a part of their little group. She'd not expected that. In fact, she'd feared they would see her as a nuisance they had to endure because she was a friend of Chandler's.

A friend. Was that really the right description for the connection between her and Chandler? Not exactly, she thought, as she munched her way through the last of the lunch Reeva had packed for her. She and Chandler weren't lovers. They weren't even boyfriend and girlfriend. Well, maybe in her mind they were, but not in reality. And yet with each passing day, she recognized her feelings for him were growing deeper and stronger. And she was helpless to stop them.

"Well, I could sit out here for at least another hour and enjoy the sunshine, but I'd better get back inside. If I don't get those orders for meds in they probably won't be shipped today."

Roslyn glanced across the wooden picnic table at Loretta, a young redheaded woman who took care of most of the clinic's paperwork. She lived some twenty-five miles north in the tiny town of Congress. She was sweet and funny and single, and Chandler often referred to her as Miss Prospector because on the weekends she went digging in creek beds, searching for a stray gold nugget.

Roslyn enjoyed the woman's company and the two of them had fallen into the habit of sharing their lunch together in the little patch of fenced-in yard behind the clinic.

"I should probably go back in, too," Roslyn said as she gathered up the remains of her lunch. "Chandler was going to return a few phone calls while the rest of us had lunch. He's probably back to seeing patients."

Loretta shook her head. "He never got to the phone calls. A few minutes ago, he left word at the front office that he and Trey were leaving on an emergency call. I don't expect them back for a while. So put up your feet and rest a few more minutes."

Roslyn smiled at her. "If you insist."

"I do," she said cheerily, then headed back into the building.

With Loretta gone, Roslyn decided to use the quiet moment to call Nikki back in Fort Worth.

As soon as she told her friend that she was presently at work, on her lunch break, a loud gasp rattled Roslyn's ear.

"Work? Are you kidding me? Doing what?"

Roslyn chuckled at the shocked tone in Nikki's voice. "No kidding, Nikki. I'm working at an animal hospital. And you can't imagine how much I'm enjoying it."

"I can't imagine you at an animal hospital, period. Just exactly what are you doing there? Working as a receptionist or in bookkeeping?"

Roslyn glanced around the small fenced-in yard. From her shaded seat, she could see a portion of the barn and connecting pens. Jimmy, the other male assistant on staff, was presently tending to a cow. As of yet, Roslyn hadn't visited the barn area, but she hoped to. She wanted to learn as much about the large animals as she did the small ones.

"No. I work back in the treatment area. Right now I'm mostly cleaning up and fetching things like medicines and bandages and things like that. I've not actually helped to treat an animal yet, but Chandler said I will soon. He says I'm learning fast."

"So this isn't just a grooming-and-kenneling business," she stated.

Roslyn had to choke back a laugh. "No. There's a real doctor here—treating life-and-death situations. In fact, Chandler just finished up a cesarian section on a beagle hound. I got to watch the whole procedure so I'm hoping next time I might get to assist him."

"Oh, yuck, you watched something that gross? How could you?"

Yes, Nikki would find it gross. As much as Roslyn had always loved her dear friend, Nikki had never been an animal-loving, outdoors type of girl. She was the girly type who was always ready to go to the mall and get her nails done. Or spend the afternoon shopping for high heels.

"Because the dog was in great distress and would've died if Chandler hadn't performed the surgery. Now the mother and pups will all be fine."

"Uh, who is this Chandler person you keep mentioning?"

The center of her universe, Roslyn thought. To Nikki, she said, "He's the vet that owns the hospital. Actually, I'm living with his family. So that's how I wound up getting the job."

"Oh. So the vet is a man?"

Roslyn sipped milk from a small carton, but found the self-discipline to keep away from the zip-locked bag of homemade snickerdoodles.

"Yes. And he's a very good vet, I might add. He sees tons of patients. Mostly cats and dogs and horses and cows. But he also treats birds and reptiles. In fact, a parrot was here this morning. Poor thing had a case of mites."

Nikki's laugh was full of disbelief. "Roslyn, listen to you! I can't believe you're into this animal thing! And why have you started work at this point in your pregnancy? You're just a week or two away from having the baby."

"One of the women on staff needed extra time off for personal reasons, so I wanted to help out. As for the timing, I still have several more days until I reach my due date. And to tell you the truth, I feel much better moving around and doing things. Actually, I've never felt better in my life."

Or more alive, Roslyn could've added. This past week since she'd begun work at the clinic, her whole world had quickly started to change.

"Well, I'll admit you've never sounded this happy," Nikki said coyly. "Does that joyous ring in your voice have anything to do with your boss?"

"My boss? You mean Chandler?"

"Yes. The vet. Tell me more about him. Is he young? Good-looking?"

Roslyn groaned. "Don't even go there, Nikki. And before you start peppering me with more questions, I'll give you this much. He's young, but older than me. And yes, he's very good-looking."

"And single?"

"Determinedly so."

Nikki chuckled knowingly. "The challenging type, huh. But aren't they all?"

Roslyn closed her eyes and tried not think about a future beyond her time with Chandler and his family. She wanted to cherish each and every day while she was here. Not picture the loneliness that would follow her to California.

She sighed. "All relationships are challenging, Nikki. Some more than others. Anyway, I don't expect to run into a man who wants to hitch himself to a single mother."

"Don't kid yourself, Ros. You're everything a man would want."

Roslyn glanced down at her burgeoning waistline and laughed. "You should see me, Nikki. I look like a watermelon."

Nikki made a scoffing sound. "You're not going to look that way for much longer. In a couple of months you're going to have that fabulous figure of yours back."

If you're thinking your thick waistline makes you any less desirable than the next woman, your thinking is all wrong.

Chandler's gently spoken words whispered through her head. He'd sounded so sincere and when he'd laid his hand on her belly and felt the baby move, she'd thought there was something akin to love on his face. But a woman could imagine anything when she was looking at a man with her heart rather than her eyes, she thought dismally.

"Hah! Two months won't get me there. But thanks for the thought, anyway." A quick glance at her watch told her she'd been talking longer than planned. "My lunch time is up, Nikki. I need to get back to work."

Nikki let out a disappointed sigh. "Okay. I'll say goodbye, even though I still have tons of questions to ask you. Like when are you coming home? And have you talked to your dad?"

Home? She'd not known what being home really meant until she'd met Chandler and moved into the ranch house on Three Rivers. But she wasn't ready to share her feelings with Nikki.

"I'm never coming back to Fort Worth. Once I get settled permanently you can fly out to see me and the baby. In fact, the baby might need her auntie to change a few diapers."

Nikki's laugh was dubious. "I should warn you that I tried changing a diaper once on my cousin's first baby. It was disastrous for me and little Caleb. But for you, dear Ros, I'll take baby-care lessons before I come for a visit."

Laughing at that, Roslyn ended the call and quickly made her way back into the clinic.

After a hurried lunch at a little roadside café in Yarnell, Chandler called the clinic to let the receptionist know he'd be returning in the next thirty minutes.

"Let me drive this time," Trey suggested, as the two men approached the black truck sitting at the edge of the dusty parking lot. "You need the rest."

Chandler responded with a short, dry laugh. "Do I look like I'm getting feeble, or something?"

"Not even close. You've had a long morning, that's all."

Chandler couldn't argue that point. He'd left the ranch before daylight and hadn't stopped until a few minutes ago to wolf down a plate of tamales and beans.

Pulling the keys from his jeans pocket, he tossed them to Trey. "Have at it. Just make sure your foot doesn't get too heavy. You don't need another speeding ticket on your record."

"Oh, Doc, I haven't had a speeding ticket in at least, uh...at least three months," he said sheepishly.

Chandler grunted. "I'd hate to be your insurance agent."

"I don't know why," Trey retorted. "He's making a small fortune off me."

They climbed into the truck and as Trey gunned it onto the highway, Chandler gave up and scooted down in the seat.

"Wake me up five miles before we reach town," Chandler told him.

"Sure, Doc. You go right ahead and get you a nice nap. You deserve it."

Closing his eyes, Chandler tilted his hat over his face.

Yet as sleep-deprived as he was, his brain wouldn't shut down. How could it? If he wasn't working he was thinking about Roslyn and wondering why he'd ever been crazy enough to kiss her. Now he wanted more than her kisses. He wanted to make love to her. He wanted to be close to her in every way a man could be close to a woman. But even if she wanted the same thing, the timing was all wrong. She was about to have the baby. And afterward? He could only guess how she might feel about him when that time arrived.

The steady hum of the motor was suddenly drowned out by the loud burst of the radio.

Chandler sat straight up and screwed his hat back onto his head. "What are you doing?"

Trey jabbed a forefinger at the radio. "Sorry, Doc, I had to turn it up. That's one of my favorite songs."

Chandler's gaze went from his grinning face to the panel on the dashboard displaying the name of the song being played by the satellite station.

His jaw dropped as he looked at Trey. "Since when did you start listening to standards?"

A grimace wrinkled Trey's lean face. "And what, may I ask, is wrong with listening to standards? Just because I wear cowboy boots caked with manure doesn't mean I can't appreciate good music. The kind with melodies and voices that are real and not manipulated with a computer."

With a shake of his head, Chandler said, "I'm amazed, Trey. Truly amazed."

"Well, I'll bet if you ask Roslyn, she'll tell you that she likes standards, too."

Chandler rolled his eyes in Trey's direction. "And how do you know this? You asked her?"

"Shoot, no! I can just tell by looking at her," Trey answered confidently. "She's all class. Nothing trashy about that woman. She has good taste."

"Guess you can tell this just by looking at her, too, huh?" Chandler asked drolly.

"Well, yeah. She has good taste in men. 'Cause it's pretty obvious that she's gone on you."

Chandler sputtered, "What the hell are you talking about? Who's been spreading that kind of rumor?"

Trey shook his head. "Calm down, Doc. No one is talking about the two of you. This is my own opinion and I won't say anything to anybody. Unless you want me to, that is."

"I want you to keep your mouth shut. Period!" Chandler suddenly boomed. "Can you do that for one blessed minute?"

Trey glanced at him, then fastened his eyes back on the highway. "Hmmph! Guess I touched a nerve."

"No. You didn't just touch a nerve," Chandler barked at him. "You've stomped on about a thousand nerves."

"Well, pardon me, for being a friend," Trey said, managing to sound sarcastic and offended at the same time. "If you think about it for a minute, it'll dawn on you that I'm the only guy you can talk to about private things. Besides your brothers, that is."

Damn if Trey wasn't right, Chandler thought. As irritating as the man could be, he was more than Chandler's working partner. He was a friend. Someone who would give his very last penny to Chandler if he thought he needed it. And though he was a chatterbox from dawn to dusk, he never repeated anything Chandler had told him in confidence.

Wiping a hand over his face, Chandler said, "Don't mind me, Trey. Here lately I've had a lot on my mind."

"You always have a lot on your mind."

"Yeah. But this is different," he muttered as he looked out the passenger window at the passing landscape. The area was as raw and untamed as much of Arizona. The stark hills were covered with outbreaks of rock mounds and brushy vegetation. Thanks to the late-winter moisture, there was green grass on some of the lower slopes, along with bursts of red and yellow wildflowers. He really should drive Roslyn through this area, he thought. She'd think it was beautiful.

"You're talking about Roslyn now."

He didn't know how the guy was so perceptive. Or was it that Chandler was so transparent? "She's part of what's on my mind," he admitted.

A different song began playing on the radio and Chandler recognized it as one that had been sung at Blake and Katherine's wedding. His oldest brother was married and had three children now. His youngest brother, Joseph, had a wife and baby with plans to add more to their brood. Both men were happier than Chandler had ever seen them. And somehow they'd learned to juggle their jobs to accommodate their family life. In Chandler's eyes they were supermen and something he could never be.

"Why?" Trey asked. "You regret letting her work at the clinic?"

Chandler had to admit she'd surprised the hell out of him this past week. She'd been doing her part to help at the clinic without one complaint about being tired. In fact, she seemed to be thoroughly enjoying everything that went on with caring for the animals. Even scrubbing soiled examination tables and cleaning dog kennels. And he'd more than enjoyed having her near.

"What's there to regret? She's loving it. And every bit she does helps Cybil keep up. It's just that—"

"She'll be having the baby soon."

"I'm looking forward to that," Chandler admitted.

"Are you? Maybe you're thinking after the baby gets here, she'll be heading on to California."

"She will be heading to California," he said, unable to keep the hollowness he was feeling from his voice. "She has a little house and piece of property there. She'll make it her home and make a new life for herself and the baby."

"Without you. That's really what's on your mind, isn't it?"

Chandler squinted a sharp look at him. "Look, Trey, Roslyn isn't my business. And I'm in no position to try and make her my business. Even though I like her…a lot."

Trey's short laugh was mocking. "Hell, Doc, don't try to kid a kidder. It just won't work. You're making a bunch of excuses because you're too afraid to try and make her your woman."

Snorting, Chandler stared blindly out the windshield. "Afraid of what?"

"Plenty of things. Like how she might turn you down. How she might rather be in California or even go back to her rich daddy in Texas rather than stay on an isolated ranch with you. Or maybe the baby's daddy is still in her heart and she doesn't have room for you in it."

Chandler felt sick inside. Because no matter how dorky Trey could get at times, the guy somehow managed to put his finger on the crux of the matter. "If you think I've gone and fallen in love with Roslyn, you're all wrong, Trey. My life is full. Too full for a wife and baby."

Trey tugged on the brim of his battered straw hat, then shot Chandler a goofy grin. "I never mentioned anything about love. You're the one who brought that up."

"So I did," Chandler muttered. "Now see if you can build a fire in this thing. You're driving at a turtle's pace."

Trey cursed. "'Slow down. Don't get a speeding ticket.

Speed up. You're going like a turtle.' This'll be the last time I drive you anywhere, Doc."

"Other than crazy, you mean?"

"No. You're doing that to yourself."

Chandler started to give him a sharp retort, but promptly bit back the words. Trey was right, he suddenly concluded. He was driving himself crazy thinking about Roslyn and the uncertainty surrounding her future plans. Did he honestly want to be a part of them? Or in the end, would he be better off to let her go?

He'd never managed to maintain a lasting relationship with a woman. Trying with Roslyn might end up breaking both their hearts. He was half out of his mind with wanting her and needing to tell her just how deeply his feelings for her had grown.

But what would happen if he did tell her? Or maybe he should be asking himself, what would happen if he didn't?

Chapter Nine

The next evening, Roslyn was giving the last of the four beagle puppies its bottle of milk when Chandler walked into the room.

"Looks like he's enjoying every drop of his supper," he said as he stood next to her shoulder and peered down at the tan-and-white puppy she was cradling in the crook of her arm.

"He's certainly nursing like he feels good," Roslyn agreed.

"You're going to make a good mother, Roslyn."

The compliment warmed her, but it was the odd light flickering in his blue eyes that was creating a slow burn in her cheeks.

Clearing her throat, she said, "Hopefully I inherited my mother's nurturing instincts. It's not something you can learn from a book."

His eyes continued to study her face. "No. It comes from within."

This was the first quiet moment Roslyn had shared with him today and as always, just standing next to him, breathing in his scent and feeling the heat radiating from his body were enough to make her knees mushy.

Drawing in a deep breath, she looked back down at the tiny puppy. "He's nearly finished. Is there something else you need for me to do?"

"Have the other pups been fed?"

She nodded. "He's the last one."

"Good. I just finished treating the final patient for the day so we're closing up," he told her. "Loretta and Danielle have already locked the front. Cybil and Violet are going to stay here at the clinic tonight and take turns with feeding the pups until morning."

There were a pair of cots in a small alcove just off the recovery room for times Chandler or other staff members were needed at the clinic throughout the night.

"Oh, my. That's every two hours!" Roslyn exclaimed. "They'll be exhausted tomorrow."

"They're tough. They're used to doing overnighters. And by tomorrow afternoon, the owner can take mother and pups home. Then it will be her responsibility to care for the new little family. Hopefully she'll have someone there to help her."

With the tiny bottle drained of the specially mixed formula, Roslyn placed the pup back with his two brothers and one sister, then carefully latched the kennel.

"I think I've finished all the chores in here and I've put up the new medicines that arrived this afternoon," she told him. "All I need to do now is gather my things from my locker."

"Uh, before you do that, Roslyn, I have something to ask you," he said.

She turned to look at him and was surprised to see a

hesitant expression on his face. One thing she'd learned about Chandler, especially since she'd been working here at the clinic, was that he never seemed uncertain or indecisive. But something was bothering him now.

"Is anything wrong, Chandler?"

"Wrong? No. Not at all." He gave her a lopsided grin, then shook his head. "I'm really rusty at this, Roslyn. What I'm trying to do is ask you to join me for dinner, here in town—just the two of us."

It was a good thing there weren't any flies in the room because Roslyn couldn't stop her mouth from falling open. "Dinner? Just you and me—like a date?"

"Well, I guess it is a date," he answered. "Do you feel up to it? Or would you rather go on home to the ranch so you can rest?"

Actually, her back had been aching off and on since she'd eaten lunch, but she wasn't about to let that stop her from sharing a special evening with Chandler.

"Oh, no. I don't want to rest. I'd love to go." She looked down at herself. "Except I don't have any other clothes with me."

"I don't, either. But we don't care if we're wearing work clothes, do we?"

She gave him a wide smile. "I don't mind at all. Just give me a minute to freshen up."

"Take your time. I'll wait for you in my office," he told her.

She hurried out of the recovery room and down the hallway to a small room furnished with lockers and a private restroom for the staff.

After plucking her handbag from a locker space, she rummaged around for a compact and tube of lipstick. With a shaky hand, she applied both, then took down her ponytail and brushed through the shoulder-length tresses.

Even with the powder and lipstick she looked rather pale, but there wasn't much she could do about that tonight. Besides, it wasn't like Chandler hadn't seen her all day in her jeans and work shirt and very little makeup.

She was turning away from the mirror, when Loretta walked into the room, then stopped and stared. "Oh, Roslyn, I thought you'd already gone for the day."

"No. I only finished feeding the baby beagles a few minutes ago." She gestured downward at her shirt and jeans. "Do I look presentable enough to go into a restaurant?"

Loretta arched an eyebrow at her. "You're staying in town for dinner?"

Roslyn felt a blush sting her cheeks. "I am. Chandler's taking me out," she said, unable to hold back the rush of excitement in her voice.

Loretta's big green eyes were suddenly glinting with speculation. "Chandler? I didn't realize you call the boss by his given name."

Which was telling, Roslyn thought. Everyone here at the clinic called him Doc. But he wasn't actually her boss. Well, maybe he was in a technical sense. But that was only a small portion of what he was to Roslyn.

Turning, Roslyn thrust the hairbrush into the handbag she'd left lying on a shelf in the open locker. "Well, that is his name," she reasoned.

"Hmm. And you have been living with him and his family. I can see why he's Chandler to you." She moved closer to Roslyn and lowered her voice to a sly whisper. "Is this dinner a real date?"

Roslyn didn't have to look in the mirror to know that her cheeks had turned an even deeper pink. "That's what he called it. I'm not willing to call it that, though."

Loretta looked at her in disbelief. "Why ever not? Doc

means what he says. Unless he's teasing. And he's not nearly as much of a jokester as his brother Holt."

"You know Holt?" Roslyn asked with faint surprise.

Loretta chuckled. "There probably isn't a woman in all of Yavapai County and beyond who doesn't know Holt Hollister."

Roslyn had heard about Holt's numerous escapades with the ladies and yet since she'd been living at Three Rivers, she'd not seen him with even one woman. She was beginning to think Holt's reputation as a ladies' man was mostly just an overblown rumor.

"Well, think what you like," Roslyn told her. "But Chandler is just being nice and feeding me before we head home. He's not really taking me on a date."

Loretta pulled an impish face at her. "If he isn't, then he should be."

Stepping back, she gave Roslyn a closer inspection. "You look fine. Except there's some sort of stain at the bottom of your shirt."

"There is? Where? I don't see anything."

"It's below your belly. That's why you can't see it." She picked up the hem of Roslyn's navy blue blouse and pulled it up high enough to show her the large stain.

"Oh, drat. I spilled some of the puppy formula when I was mixing it. I guess it went on my shirt, too."

Loretta suddenly snapped her fingers. "Not to worry. I just now remembered I have something in my locker you can wear."

Roslyn laughed out loud. "Are you crazy? I couldn't squeeze myself into any of your blouses."

"You can this one. It's one of those flowy, filmy things that's way too feminine for me. My mother gave it to me as a gift. Her way of saying you need to look more alluring. I brought it to work thinking I was going to take it back to the store for an exchange. I never did. And here it still hangs."

She pulled the garment out of the locker next to Roslyn's and held it out for her to see.

Roslyn instantly gasped with delight at the coral-and-yellow printed blouse. "Oh, how pretty! And the way it's cut, maybe I could get in it. Are you sure you won't mind if I wear it?"

"I'd love it if you would. Here, let me help with the buttons. You don't want to keep Doc waiting."

Chandler was trying to keep his eyes on the street and the slow-moving car in front of him, but every few seconds he found himself glancing over at Roslyn.

How she'd instantly transformed herself he didn't know, but somehow she'd managed to make herself look particularly lovely tonight. And not just because Loretta had lent her a blouse. Her face seemed to be radiating a special light and her brown eyes were glowing with… what? Was that love? Happiness? Whatever it was, he wanted some of it.

"Is there a particular kind of food you'd like to eat tonight? Since Wickenburg is small there's not a whole lot of choices, but most of them are good," he told her.

"I like all kinds of food. You pick. This is your town. You know what's best."

Chandler had never dated what he'd considered snobbish women. But after Roslyn's agreeable comment, he realized that none of them had been as accommodating as she was. Not just about the choice of a restaurant, but about everything. All of them would've been insulted if he'd asked them on a date fifteen minutes ahead of time. And they would've definitely suggested he drive on down to Phoenix so they could have a *real* dinner served to them."

"Okay. I think I know a place you might like. We'll be there in five minutes."

"Town seems busy this evening," she remarked as she gazed out at the shops and businesses lining the street.

"It's Friday. Folks are getting ready for the weekend."

She glanced over at him. "I've never noticed you doing anything special on the weekend."

He shrugged a shoulder. "I used to do plenty of things on the weekend. Especially with my brothers. We'd go over to Lake Pleasant and fish. And once in a while we'd drive up to Cliff Castle. That's a casino up near Camp Verde. Holt usually made a killing at the blackjack tables."

She laughed. "That's not surprising. And what about you?"

He chuckled. "I mostly watched Holt. That way I saved my money."

She turned her knees so that she was facing him. "So what about now? You don't ever do those types of things anymore?"

He shook his head. "No. And I can't exactly tell you why. Except that after Dad died, I guess all of us began to change in some ways. So did the ranch. Suddenly everything turned serious and we all decided that making sure it remained in the black and keeping the Hollister legacy going was more important than anything."

"You weren't thinking in those terms when your father was alive?"

"Up to a certain point. Don't get me wrong, we all worked hard back then. But with Dad around we never doubted or worried about the ranch's solvency. He was our rock. Losing him shook all of us. And it hit Blake the hardest. He threw every bit of himself into the ranch and suffered a broken engagement because of it. For a long time Joe was driven to find Dad's killer. Every spare moment he had was spent on solving the case. And Holt, well, he just went a little wilder with the women and horses and whiskey."

"And you? What about you, Chandler?" she asked gently.

He rubbed a hand over his face. "These past six years since Dad died, I've tried not to think about my life too much. But now that you're here, I'm beginning to see there's more for me than the ranch and my patients." He reached over and clasped her hand in his. "I've told you this before, but I'll say it again. I'm very glad you decided to park in front of the clinic that first night you hit town."

As his fingers warmed her hand, she felt her heart melting into a helpless little puddle.

Smiling at him, she said, "I'm kinda glad I did, too."

Jose's, the restaurant Chandler chose for their evening meal, was located on the edge of town and far enough from the main highway to make it a quiet and cozy spot.

The building was fashioned in a sprawling, hacienda style with stucco walls painted a pale turquoise and a red tiled roof. A porch with arched supports ran the width of the front and at the top of each arch hung long strings of drying red peppers. At one end of the porch, a bougainvillea covered in yellow-gold blossoms grew all the way to the roof, while at the opposite end a single saguaro stood like a sentinel against the desert horizon.

Roslyn was totally charmed by the outside of the place and even more so when they entered the small restaurant and took seats in a quiet corner. All through the meal of avocado stuffed with grilled chicken, she continued to gaze around at the little round tables with orange-and-white checked tablecloths and vases of yellow marigolds.

"This is so nice, Chandler. Thank you for inviting me out tonight and bringing me to this beautiful little place. Don't tell Reeva, but the food is out-of-this-world delicious. And speaking of Reeva, I hope you called to let her know we wouldn't be eating at home tonight."

"I called. And she didn't even yell at me," he joked. "I suspect that after the big group she had for dinner last night, she was relieved to get a break."

Roslyn smiled as she sliced her fork into a piece of *tres leches* cake. "Last night was a surprise for me. No one had told me Joe and his family, and your sister, Vivian, and her family, were going to show up for dinner. I really enjoyed visiting with all of them."

Candler grinned. "I think you especially liked Little Joe."

Laughing softly, Roslyn shook her finger at him. "Tessa says everyone has to start leaving off the little part of his name or he'll forever be known as Little Joe instead of Joseph Junior."

"Hah! I have news for my sister-in-law. It's too late to drop the little. That part of my nephew's name has already stuck."

She swallowed another bite of cake. "You're probably right. But no matter what name you call him, Joe is adorable. And I'll tell you another thing. If my child is a girl, I hope she grows up to be as lovely and vivacious as Hannah. She and Nick are quite a pair together, aren't they?"

She probably wasn't aware of it, Chandler thought, but Roslyn had become a part of the family, too. But would she want to remain a part of it? She'd already left her home and her father back in Texas. What made Chandler think he'd be able to hold her at Three Rivers?

Not wanting to dwell on that question tonight, he tried to push it out of his head and focus strictly on her and this rare time of being alone with her.

"Hannah and Nick have a special bond," he answered. "From the first time those two kids met, they hit it off perfectly. Which surprised the heck out of me. Nick is about a year or two younger than Hannah and for a long time she tended to boss him around, but he seemed to like it. Now that Hannah lives on the reservation, they don't get to see each other every day. But their parents make sure the two of them still get to spend plenty of time together."

Roslyn nodded. "Katherine told me that one of the reasons Nick and Hannah clicked so much was that neither had a father."

"That's true. Kat's first husband died in a car accident and Vivian's ex never had any desire to be a father to Hannah. Fortunately, both kids have two parents now. Blake is a good father to Nick and Sawyer is a great dad to Hannah. So everybody is happy."

She let out a wistful sigh as her gaze drifted down to the last of her dessert. "When I first ended my engagement I didn't dwell too much on my baby not having a father. But here lately it's been on my mind much more. Now that the baby is nearly here I feel guilty. My child isn't even born yet and I've already failed him, or her."

He'd never heard her talk this way and it cut into him more than he wanted to admit. She'd been duped and betrayed by a man who'd never deserved her in the first place. Chandler didn't want her to carry around a load of guilt or hurt for any reason.

Reaching across the table, he wrapped his hand around hers. "You shouldn't be feeling guilty. Just think about it. Do you think your baby would be better off with a father who's a liar and a cheat? I don't."

Beneath the veil of her long lashes, her brown eyes studied his face until a glaze of tears suddenly threatened to spill onto her cheeks. Then she glanced away and swallowed hard.

"I know you're right about that. But that doesn't make me any less of a failure." She turned her gaze back onto his face. "I should've had better judgment. I shouldn't have wanted to please my father so much and followed my heart instead."

Her last words caught his attention. "You mean there was someone you loved before Erich, but your father didn't find him suitable?"

She shook her head. "No. Before Erich I never had any serious feelings about a guy. There were a few, if given a chance, I might've fallen in love with. But they were regular men with regular jobs. Being *regular* never stacked up good enough for Martin DuBose."

What did she consider Chandler? Just a mediocre country vet? Or was she thinking the Hollisters were too wealthy for her taste? Most folks would probably consider that to be a crazy question, but he didn't. He'd noticed that Roslyn never talked about her family's wealth, or the things it could get for her. He wasn't at all sure that she even liked being wealthy.

"You'll fall in love soon enough and give your child a father." The words coming out of his mouth sounded stiff and awkward. And why shouldn't they? Just thinking about Roslyn being in another man's arms made him sick, through and through.

She pushed aside the dessert plate and picked up her coffee cup. "We're always talking about me, Chandler. What about you?"

"Me?" He shrugged nonchalantly. "My life is already settled. There's not much to talk about."

Her head moved slowly back and forth. "I don't believe that."

"Which part?"

She grimaced. "The part about your life already being settled. I can't imagine you spending the remainder of your years without a wife, or babies, or time for yourself."

He cleared his throat. She was giving him the opportunity to make a statement. He could ease his hand away from hers and flatly explain that he didn't want any of those things. But the truth was, he'd be lying. Deep down he wanted to be like his married brothers. He wanted to experience that same joy and love that they were blessed with each and every day.

"To be honest, Roslyn, having those things used to be one of my main goals. While I was in vet school I came close to asking a woman to marry me. But that didn't work out. My studies took up too much of my time. Then later, after I'd started my own clinic, I met a woman I thought might be *the* one. She had her own career as a nurse. She understood about putting in long, irregular hours at work. And she was as dedicated to her profession as I was to mine."

"What happened?"

"Actually, I had driven to Phoenix to find the perfect diamond engagement ring to give her when she called and said we needed to talk. You know, the old phrase that basically means 'I'm dumping you.'"

"But why? Had she found someone else?"

"No. At least I didn't have to bear that humiliation. She was honest enough to tell me that she'd never be happy living on the ranch, making a sixty- or seventy-mile commute to work every day. She wasn't an outdoor girl. Nor was she an animal lover, so basically there was nothing at Three Rivers that appealed to her."

Her eyes softened and her fingers squeezed his. "There was you."

If the long room hadn't been filled with evening diners, he would have leaned across the table and kissed her. As it was, he could merely gaze at her and wish.

"Uh, well, I wasn't enough. You see, I don't think she ever really loved me. She dated me in hopes that I was the right one. But I wasn't."

She let out a long breath, then flexed her shoulders. "It's good that you didn't make a mistake with either of them. But time has passed and I think..."

A grimace wrinkled her brow as she pulled her hand from his and rubbed it against the small of her back.

"What's wrong?" Chandler asked with sudden concern. "Are you not feeling well?"

"I don't feel sick. This afternoon twinges started coming and going in my lower back. I thought that once I got off my feet the pains would quit. But to be honest, they're getting worse."

"I'd better pay out. I think the baby is coming," he told her.

Her mouth popped open, very nearly making Chandler laugh outright.

"The baby? But it can't be! It's still several days until my due date. And I just went for a checkup two days ago."

"Didn't he tell you the baby could come early or late?"

She bit down on her lower lip. "Well, yes, he did say that. But—"

She didn't finish speaking. Instead, she groaned and grabbed her back with both hands.

Chandler promptly signaled to the waiter and after explaining the situation gave him a very large bill to cover the meal and a generous tip.

With his arm around Roslyn's waist, Chandler helped her outside and into the truck.

As he steered the truck in the direction of the hospital, she gave him a wobbly smile.

"I'm so sorry I've cut our evening short, Chandler. It's the nicest date I've ever been on," she told him.

She was doing her best to smile through her pain and all of a sudden Chandler's heart was so full of feelings for this woman he wondered if it might burst.

"It's the nicest one I've ever been on, too," he said, his voice sounding like his throat had been sandpapered. "We'll do it again. After the baby gets here and you're back on your feet. Is that a date?"

Nodding, she clutched the front of her stomach. "It's a date, Doc."

Chapter Ten

Since Maureen had already promised Roslyn she'd be with her in the delivery room, Chandler gave his mother a quick call as he made the short drive to the hospital.

Unfortunately, the call went straight to her voice mail so he called the line in the kitchen, figuring Reeva would be sure to answer.

"Chandler, what are you doing on the phone?" She fired the question at him before he had a chance to get one word out. "You're supposed to be taking Roslyn out to dinner!"

"We've already had dinner. I'm taking her to the hospital. Is Mom in the house? She's not answering her phone."

"No. She's still out with the hands. They decided to move some of the cattle down from Prescott today. It'll probably be after midnight before she gets back," the cook explained, then practically shouted in his ear. "Did you say hospital? Is Roslyn having the baby?"

"Looks like it. And Mom was planning on being her labor coach," he explained. "Now it looks—"

"Coach, hell!" Reeva interrupted with a snort. "Roslyn doesn't need a coach at her side. She needs a man! Don't you think you fit the bill?"

Chandler had tended hundreds of animal births. Many had been easy, while a few had ended tragically. Throughout, he'd determinedly kept a calm, level head because he was the man who was responsible for helping the new little lives enter the world. But none of them had been human. None of them had been the woman who'd grabbed onto his heart and now held it in the palm of her hands.

"I'll try, Reeva. Leave Mom a message, will you?"

"She'll get the message. And I'll call upstairs right now and let Blake and Kat know what's going on."

"Thanks, Reeva."

Chandler ended the call and finished the short drive to the hospital in record time. By the time he wheeled the truck into the emergency-room entrance and parked beneath a wide overhang, Roslyn was already experiencing contractions.

He lifted her out of the seat and began carrying her toward the sliding glass doors, when a dark-haired nurse wearing navy blue scrubs met them with a wheelchair.

"Has she started labor?" she asked.

"It appears so," Chandler answered as he gently deposited Roslyn into the chair, then stepped out of the way.

The nurse wheeled Roslyn into the building while Chandler was left to follow. Along the way, the woman peppered Roslyn with pertinent health questions and Chandler was content to remain silent and allow the woman to take control. Until she parked the wheelchair in front of an admissions desk.

"What are you doing?" He was boiling over with frustration. "There isn't time for this. Roslyn is in labor! She needs care, not questions!"

"I'm sorry, Mr., uh— I don't believe you've told me your name," the nurse stated calmly.

He took note of the name tag pinned to the left shoulder of her scrub top. Mariana Reed.

"My name is Hollister, Ms. Reed. Dr. Chandler Hollister," he said with what little patience he could summon.

Most everyone in the area recognized the Hollister name. Along with owning and operating Three Rivers, the family donated large sums of money to different local causes in the community, including this very hospital. But the skeptical arch to Nurse Reed's eyebrows made him think she doubted he was actually a Hollister or a doctor.

Apparently she thought he should be dressed in a tailored suit and wingtips instead of a cowboy who'd been in one too many feed lots.

Nurse Reed loudly cleared in throat. "Well, Dr. Hollister, in your profession you should know the hospital has to have your wife's necessary information before we can treat her. If you can provide it and her insurance card, I'll be happy to take her on back to the labor room."

There was long list of things he wanted to tell the nurse. The main one being that if he waited around for paperwork to be completed, most of his patients would die before he ever got the chance to treat them.

Chandler opened his mouth to give Nurse Reed a sharp retort, but by then Roslyn had recovered enough to interrupt the exchange. She reached for his hand and squeezed it as though he was the one who needed reassuring rather than her.

"Chandler, it's okay," she said. "The last time I visited

the doctor, Kat brought me by the hospital so I could fill out preadmission papers. Everything should be ready to go."

The nurse promptly instructed an older lady sitting at the admission desk to check for the information. After Roslyn supplied her birthdate and social security number, the clerk confirmed that the necessary info had already been registered.

With a smug smile for Chandler, the nurse said, "Looks like your wife already has things under control. So if you'd like to follow us down the hallway, there's a waiting room on the left, where you can make yourself comfortable while we take care of your wife."

"Oh, but can't he come with me?" Roslyn asked anxiously.

"Not right now," the nurse answered with a shake of her head. "He may come back later on, after we get you settled in a labor room."

Roslyn glanced up at Chandler and the beseeching look in her eyes tore a hole right through his heart. "You will stay with me, won't you?"

"Wild horses couldn't drag me away," he promised.

Nurse Reed's stern expression softened with approval. "Now that's the way a husband should be talking to the woman who's about to give him a child."

Roslyn looked awkwardly from Chandler to the nurse. "But he's not my husband," she explained.

The confession caused the nurse to pierce Chandler with a look of real disappointment. If she was trying to make him feel like a heel, she was doing a great job of it, he decided. But he'd rather have the nurse thinking he was a jerk, rather than put Roslyn through the awkward explanation of her broken engagement.

"I should have guessed," Nurse Reed said bluntly. "Then you—"

"I'm the baby's father." The quick claim spurted out of Chandler's mouth before he could even think about the consequences. "And I want to be present at the birth."

If the nurse was surprised to hear that a member of the Hollister family was having a child out of wedlock, she didn't show it. Instead, she merely nodded.

"Certainly, Dr. Hollister, I'll let you know when you can join her."

Relieved, he bent down and placed a kiss on Roslyn's cheek. "I'll see you in a few minutes, darling."

A look of confusion filled her eyes, but pain quickly followed and before he had a chance to say more, the nurse was wheeling her away.

As Chandler watched her go, he felt a big part of himself going with her.

Five hours later, Roslyn gave birth to a perfect little daughter. Exhausted and exhilarated at the same time, tears streamed down her cheeks when the delivery room finally calmed and the baby was placed upon her chest.

"Oh, my," she whispered in awed wonder "You're so beautiful, my baby daughter. So utterly beautiful."

She kissed the top of the baby's damp head, then glanced up to see Chandler standing at the side of her bed, where he'd been ever since they'd entered the delivery room.

Smiling at him through her tears, she said, "Come closer, Chandler, so you can see her better."

He bent over the bed railing and touched a finger to a bit of hair stuck to the newborn's scalp. As Roslyn studied his reaction, she decided he looked as overwhelmed as she felt.

"Her eyes are squinted," she said. "I can't really tell what color they are. Can you?"

Her daughter was awake and squirming, but her face was squinched as though she was getting ready to let out a loud howl.

"I've heard all babies had blue eyes."

"I don't think that's true. But maybe they are blue. Like yours," she added impishly.

A sheepish grin twisted his lips. "I hope you didn't mind me telling Nurse Reed that I was the father. I thought it would make things easier for you—and me."

How could he think she would mind? Just hearing him claim the baby as his had caused her heart to swell with emotions she could no longer deny.

"I didn't mind," she whispered. "I was…very grateful."

His gaze met hers and for a brief moment she thought he was going to kiss her, but the nearby voices of the attending nurses seemed to remind him that they weren't alone.

His attention returned to the baby. "She's incredible, Ros. Just like her mother. And I told you it was going to be a girl, didn't I?"

The teasing smile on his face added to the warm emotions spilling from her heart and spreading to every corner of her body. "You most certainly did. I'll never doubt your diagnoses again."

He chuckled then lowered his head to place a kiss on her forehead. With one hand holding the baby securely to her breasts, she reached up with her free hand to touch the side of his face.

"Thank you, Chandler, for…being here with me. For—" Tears choked her throat and she struggled to swallow away the aching lump. "For caring about me… and the baby."

His blue eyes gentle, he stroked a tangled strand of hair back from her face. "You don't have to thank me, Ros. This is where I wanted to be. We just didn't know this was going to happen on our date night, did we?"

"No. It's a date I'll never forget." For plenty of reasons, she thought. Even before the baby had decided to suddenly make her appearance into the world, Roslyn had felt Chandler drawing closer to her. Now, going through five hours of exhausting labor with him holding her hand, wiping her brow and giving her soft words of encouragement, she knew for certain that she felt more than close to him. She loved him. Plain and simple.

But where was that love going to land her? Smack in the middle of a heartache?

No. She wasn't going to try to answer that now. At this moment she was the happiest woman alive. Her child was safely born and snuggled in her arms. And whether Chandler would ever love her or not, he cared enough to be at her side at the most important time in her life. For now, she couldn't ask for more.

Before the night was over, Chandler ended up grabbing a couple of hours of sleep on a couch in the waiting room. When he woke up just before daylight, he quickly slapped water on his face and hurried to the gift shop on the bottom floor of the hospital. After purchasing the biggest bouquet of flowers he could find, he took the elevator up to Roslyn's private room, which was located in the maternity ward of the hospital.

At the door he knocked lightly, then stepped inside to see Roslyn sitting up in bed with the baby in her arms.

And from the way she'd positioned the thin blanket, he had to assume she was breast-feeding her new daughter.

"Hello," he said. "Is it okay if I come in?"

She'd brushed her light brown hair and pulled it into a ponytail, and a bit of color had been dabbed on her lips. After the hard labor she'd gone through, he didn't know where she'd found the energy to do either. But this morning she looked amazingly beautiful and refreshed.

"It's very okay. Are those for me?" she asked, her gaze going to the vase of flowers he was carrying.

"They are. Congratulations, new mother." He deposited the vase in an out-of-the-way spot on the nightstand.

"Thank you," she said. "I've never seen daisies and roses mixed together. They're very beautiful."

"So are you." He lifted off his hat, then dropped a kiss on top of Roslyn's head. "How are you feeling?"

Her smile was like a beam of sunshine and Chandler realized that seeing her happy made his spirits soar.

"After all the pain and pushing and straining, I should feel awful, I suppose. But I actually feel wonderful. I want to sing and shout."

"And so you should," Chandler said gently. "You've been blessed with a beautiful daughter. How does that feel?"

She glanced down at the baby and Chandler couldn't miss the love and pride swimming in her eyes.

"I never thought it would be like this, Chandler. I didn't know I could love this much, or feel so fiercely protective." Her eyes glistened as they met his. "But to be honest, I'm a little scared, too. I'm responsible for someone other than myself now."

He reached over and squeezed her shoulder. "You're going to be everything this little girl needs."

Now that the baby was actually here, Chandler's protective feelings for Roslyn and her child had grown to enormous proportions. And in spite of being exhausted, he'd had trouble staying asleep for more than fifteen minutes at a time. And the problem hadn't been the hard couch or the freezing temperature of the waiting room. No, his mind had been whirling with thoughts of Roslyn, the baby and how much he wanted them to remain in his life.

At this moment, with her soft brown eyes delving into his, the idea of telling her exactly how he felt was pushing and prodding at him. Yet he held back. Too much had happened in the past twenty-four hours and far more needed to happen before they could talk about a future together.

Clearing his throat, he rolled up the brim of his hat with both hands and squeezed the expensive felt. "Have you decided on a name yet?"

"I have. That is, if you agree to it."

Confused, he shook his head. "Me? What I think shouldn't matter."

She reached beneath the blanket and straightened her clothing, then slipped it away from the newborn's face. Chandler's heart instantly squeezed with love as he stared at the baby. What little hair she possessed had dried to the same light brown color as her mother's. Most of the redness had left her face and now that her features were relaxed in sleep, he decided she resembled Roslyn.

"But it does," she said. "I'd like to name her Evelyn Kay."

His gaze flew up to meet Roslyn's. "Evelyn is mother's first name. You want to name her after Mom?"

Nodding, she said, "I hope she or none of the family will mind."

He suddenly smiled. "Mind? Mom will be thrilled. If you haven't already guessed, she loves you like a daughter. But how did you know that was her name? She's always gone by Maureen."

"I was in the kitchen one day helping Reeva and we were discussing names. She told me. Kay was my mother's middle name. So she's going to be named after two special women."

"Well, I think Evelyn Kay is perfect." It would be even more perfect if the name was followed by Hollister, but that was a different matter. One that would require a commitment he wasn't sure either of them was ready to make.

He made a point of glancing at his watch. "I better go. The girls have already opened the clinic. I need to get over there," he told her.

Nodding that she understood, she smiled. "You can announce Evelyn's arrival to everyone. And in case you don't remember the nurse telling us in the delivery room, she weighed six pounds and ten ounces and she's nineteen inches long."

"And she's very beautiful, like her mother," he added with a playful wink. "I'll be sure and spread the word."

He started to leave, but before he could turn away from the bed, she quickly caught him by the hand.

Arching a brow at her, he asked, "Was there something you needed before I go?"

"No. I, uh, I just wanted to tell you that…well, that you made Evelyn's birth very special for me. I'll never forget that, Chandler."

Was this the beginning of a goodbye? No. Somehow, someway, he couldn't let that happen.

Bending, he placed a kiss on her lips."

More than two weeks later, Chandler knocked on the door of his mother's office and without waiting for an answer, stepped inside.

She was sitting at the desk with the landline phone jammed to her ear. As soon as she spotted Chandler, she motioned for him to stay and he took a seat, while she finished the phone conversation.

"I know. Yes. I'm doing the best that I can," she said. "It's not something—"

She paused and Chandler noticed a mixture of sadness and frustration on her face.

"Okay. I'm going to try not to ponder on it too much. No. Don't do that. I'll call you. Tomorrow evening." She hung up the receiver back on its hook. "Sorry about that, son. Were you wanting to talk with me?"

He couldn't tamp down his curiosity. It was nearing midnight. Who could she be talking to at this hour? "Was that Vivian or Camille?"

Instead of looking at him, she studied the ink blotter on the desktop. "No. Just someone I'm thinking of doing cattle business with. Nothing important."

She glanced up, and though Chandler hated to think it, she wasn't being truthful. Which made no sense at all. His mother wasn't a person who lied about anything. Unless she believed the lie would save someone a heartache.

Deciding not to press her on the issue for now, Chandler said, "I see. Someone on West Coast time. Well, do you have a minute to talk?"

"Always," she said. "Is anything wrong?"

Chandler didn't waste time coming to the point. "Yes. Something is very wrong. I just left Roslyn's room and she tells me she's rented an apartment in town. She's going to be moving in by midweek."

Maureen leaned back and folded her hands together in her lap. "I already know about that."

"Surely you don't approve! She needs to stay here on

the ranch, where Reeva and Jazelle and Kat can all help her with the baby."

"And you told her all of this?" Maureen asked.

"I told her that and a lot more. She has no earthly reason to get an apartment. Not when she's more than welcome to stay right here."

"I've already made that argument with her, Chandler. I'm afraid she has her mind made up. And to tell you the truth, now that I've had time to think on it, I believe she's doing the right thing for herself and the baby."

Chandler jumped straight up and began to pace around the shadowy room. "How could you say that, Mom? I can see how close you've already grown to baby Evelyn. And I know how you feel about Roslyn. You can't want them to leave!" he argued.

She frowned. "I didn't say anything about wanting them to leave. I said it was probably the best thing for them."

"Hell, what's the difference? Either way, they'll be out of the house," he muttered.

"And that bothers you."

Maureen hadn't bothered to put her words into question form. She already knew how he felt.

Shaking his head, he crossed the room and sank into the chair he'd vacated moments ago. "Damn right it bothers me. She doesn't need to be alone."

"Lots of single mothers care for their babies alone. And Roslyn isn't a helpless person. In fact, I'm very proud of her. She's taken to motherhood like a real pro. Like she's already had three or four babies before this one. I have no doubt the two of them will be fine on their own. And even if she does need some help, all she has to do is pick up the phone and one of us will be there for her. It's not like she's moving to another state."

But this is the first step to making that big move, Chandler thought. The very one he didn't want her to make.

"I don't like it."

Maureen's smile was placating. "No. I don't expect that you do. All of us can see that you've—grown very fond of Roslyn. It's understandable that you want to keep her here—close to you."

He darted a sheepish look at her. "Are my feelings for Roslyn that transparent?"

Her smile deepened. "They aren't on your sleeve yet, but they're pretty darn close."

Chandler groaned. These past couple of weeks since she'd come home with the baby he'd purposely made time away from the clinic to be with her and Evelyn. With each day that had passed, he'd fallen more and more in love with them.

"I might as well admit it, Mom. I'm crazy about her and Evelyn. But I don't know what to do about it."

She shook her head. "A good start would be telling her how you feel. Have you done that?"

He pushed fingers into his hair and raked them backward. "Not exactly. I wanted to give her time—to adjust to being a mother. And to being away from her father and home in Fort Worth. Besides, I'm not keen on being rejected."

Maureen's chuckle was full of disbelief. "I can't see that happening. Roslyn thinks you're the grandest thing since the discovery of fire. But I do think she has her doubts about you."

Stunned, Chandler stared at his mother. "What are you talking about? I've always tried to be a responsible man."

"Depends on how you define *responsible*." She stacked several papers together, then slipped them into the bottom drawer of the desk. "Yes, you're accountable to your family, the ranch and your work. But what about Roslyn and baby Evelyn?"

He groaned. "Hell, Mom? I'm giving them all the time I can."

"Right now, you are. But Roslyn doesn't know if that will last. She's already had one man upend her life. Understandably, she's going to be cautious. You need to respect her wishes to be on her own and give her time to figure everything out for herself."

Chandler was about to retort that there was no need for Roslyn to be independent. That he'd be only too happy to take care of her. But it suddenly dawned on him that he was being an idiot. Roslyn had just run away from a controlling man. He didn't want to give her reason to run again.

"You're right, Mom. But I worry..."

Maureen walked around the desk to stand in front of him.

"You worry about what?" she urged.

Frustration put a curse word on his tongue, but he bit it back. "This deal with her father. Roslyn still hasn't talked to him. You'd think she'd at least want to tell him that the baby had arrived safely and he was now the grandfather to a daughter. But she's stubborn about it."

Surprised, Maureen asked, "You brought all of that up with Roslyn?"

Chandler blew out a weary breath. "Once. Not that it did any good. She quickly shut me down."

Maureen laid a hand on his shoulder. "Chandler, not everyone's dad is as loving and supportive as the one you had. Remember that and try to respect Roslyn's wishes."

He shook his head. "Mom, you always taught us kids

that bitterness was the same as poison. To carry it around made a person sick. Don't you still believe that?"

She slowly eased into the chair next to his and rubbed her eyes with both hands. The disenchanted gesture made Chandler want to put his arm around her shoulders and remind her that he and the rest of her children hadn't forgotten the loss she'd endured.

"Dear Lord, Chandler, sometimes it amazes me how much like Joel you are." She dropped her hands and gave him a battle-weary smile. "Ever since your dad died I've tried very hard not to be bitter. But sometimes when I forget to hold my guard up, the resentful feelings creep up on me. When that happens I'm not good and…well, perhaps you're right about Roslyn. Maybe it would be best if she confronted her father and cleared the air. I can't say. But I am sure of one thing. You'll regret it if you let her get away."

On that count, Chandler couldn't argue with his mother. Roslyn and baby Evelyn had become everything to him. And somehow, someway, he had to convince her that she needed him in her life as much as he needed the two of them.

Chapter Eleven

Leaving Three Rivers had been the hardest thing Roslyn had ever done in her entire life. When she'd driven away with Evelyn and all their personal belongings, she'd felt as though a part of her heart was being torn away. The Hollisters had become her family and Chandler... Just thinking about him put a lump of emotion in her throat and filled her heart with a longing that refused to go away.

Now, after more than two weeks of being gone from the ranch and living in her own apartment, she was still questioning her decision to leave a place where she and the baby had been totally surrounded by people who cared about her.

But from the very beginning, Roslyn had made an agreement with Maureen that she would only stay until she'd had the baby and was recuperated enough to move on. That time had come and she'd been determined not to stay longer and take advantage of the generous family, even though Chandler had put up an argument for her to stay.

But it hadn't been the kind of argument Roslyn had hoped or wished to hear from him. He'd never once mentioned the word *love.* He'd never once told her that he didn't want to live without her and Evelyn. That's all it would've taken to keep her there on the ranch with him. But he'd never spoken anything that could have been construed as a vow of love. He'd not hinted anything about wanting to make a future with her. Instead, he'd kept harping on the fact that she needed to stay on the ranch, where she'd have plenty of help with the baby.

Sighing, she glanced down at Evelyn to see she'd finished nursing and had fallen asleep. Roslyn eased her nipple away from the baby's slack mouth and readjusted her clothing before she rose from the wooden rocker and placed her in a white bassinet.

At the rate her daughter was growing, it wouldn't be long before the bassinet would be too small to accommodate her. But for now, Roslyn preferred to have the baby sleeping in the same bedroom with her, instead of across the hall in the nursery.

The apartment Roslyn had rented was in an older building complex located fairly close to the school where Katherine worked as a secretary. From a window at the back of her living room, she could see a portion of a small city park equipped with gym sets and bumpy slides. At the front of the ground-floor apartment, there was a cluster of Joshua trees and a small flower bed filled with native rocks and a variety of succulents.

It was a pretty place in a quiet neighborhood and Roslyn liked the way the rooms were coming together. Since she'd moved in, she'd been gradually collecting pieces of furniture and rugs and wall decorations to make the place feel more like home. And the nursery was turning out to be bright and cheery with all white furniture and bright yellow curtains.

Yes, she and Evelyn were in their own little home now, she thought, as she walked out to the living room. This was what she'd planned from the very beginning. And no, Wickenburg was still a far distance from Redding. But that would come later.

How much later, Roslyn? When Evelyn gets to be three or four months old? Or will it take a year for you to find the courage to move on from the Hollisters—mainly one Hollister? The gentle veterinarian with black hair and sky-blue eyes and a smile that melts your bones. You need to forget Chandler. Sure, he likes your company. But he's never going to be serious. He's never going to love you.

Doing her best to shake away the mocking voice in her head, she walked into the kitchen with the intention of preparing something for the evening meal. She wasn't hungry, but she needed to make sure she maintained plenty of milk for Evelyn.

She was rummaging through the packages and cans stacked on the pantry shelf when the doorbell jangled.

Thinking it might be Katherine stopping by on her way home from work, she hurried out to the tiny foyer at the front entrance and peered through the peephole on the door. But instead of Katherine it was Chandler standing on the small, concrete porch.

This was the third visit he'd made to the apartment and each time the sight of him never failed to shoot a beam of joy right through. Even if he didn't love her, even if it was impossible for him to make a commitment to her, she wanted to be near him for as much and as long as possible. Maybe that made her foolish, but she couldn't help it.

Swinging the door wide, she greeted him with a bright hello.

"Would you like an uninvited visitor?" he asked.

The lopsided grin on his face put a smile on hers and she reached for his hand and tugged him across the threshold.

"You never need an invitation," she told him.

He held up a large brown bag in one hand and a pink paper gift sack with handles in the other. "I brought Evelyn a gift. And dinner for us," he said. "I hope you haven't already eaten."

He handed the gift to her and she peered inside to see an adorable little dress of white-and-pink checks trimmed with white lace.

"Chandler, you shouldn't have bought Evelyn anything. The nursery is already stacked with stuffed animals and toys that you've given her."

He waved away her protest. "Little girls love clothes. She can't have too many."

Groaning, Roslyn shook her head. "She's only a bit over a month old. She doesn't know what she's wearing."

Chandler chuckled. "Years from now when she sees pictures of herself, she'll be glad."

The delicious smells coming from the bag made her mouth water. Now that Chandler was here she was suddenly very hungry and very happy.

"I was just in the kitchen wondering what I was going to make myself for dinner. You've saved me from the task." She motioned for him to follow her. "Let's take that to the kitchen. Or we could eat in the dining room. The view from the table there is much nicer."

"The dining table is fine with me. But I'm not going to eat a bite until I see my baby Evelyn," he said. "Is she asleep?"

"Yes. I just put her in the bassinet. But you won't disturb her."

After Chandler deposited the sack in the kitchen, the two of them made their way to Roslyn's bedroom. Along the way, she noticed his jeans and dark brown shirt were clean, telling her he must have changed at the clinic before he'd driven over here. This evening he looked even more handsome than usual, making it very difficult for her to keep her hands off him.

Inside the bedroom, he bent over the bassinet. "Look at her! She's growing like crazy!"

"It's only been three days since you've seen her," Roslyn pointed out. "She couldn't look that much different."

"She does to me. She's gaining weight and getting longer. Next thing we know, she'll be trying to climb out of this thing!"

Roslyn didn't miss how he'd used the word *we* in his statement. And ridiculous or not, it gave her hope that he was looking toward the future. A future with her and Evelyn.

Laughing softly, Roslyn said, "She won't be able to climb for months!"

"Who says? She might be a little superwoman." He straightened and slipped his arms around Roslyn's waist, which was growing slimmer every day. "Like her mom."

Although Chandler had been showing her more and more physical affection since Evelyn had been born, he'd always pulled back before things got heated. She wasn't sure if his reticence was because she'd been recuperating from giving birth, or because he wanted to keep a cautious distance between them. Either way, each time he touched her, she felt as if every cell in her body was glowing.

"Hmm. How does it feel to be in a house with two superwomen in it?" she asked.

A low, sexy chuckle passed his lips before he lowered his head toward hers. Anticipation hummed through her as she splayed her hands on his broad chest and tilted her face up to his.

His kiss was warm and left the taste of promise on her lips. When he lifted his head, she instantly wanted to pull it back down to hers and kiss him a second time. But she didn't want to press him. She wanted him to reach for her on his own.

With a hand on his arm, she said, "Our dinner is getting cold. We'd better go eat before Evelyn decides her nap is over."

She thought she saw a flash of frustration in his blue eyes, but then he smiled and nodded. "Right. You need to eat without interruption."

As it turned out, Evelyn woke before Roslyn finished all the food on her plate. But Chandler was only too happy to go fetch the crying baby for her.

He rose from the dining-room chair. "You stay put. I'll take care of Evelyn."

"But her diaper probably needs to be changed."

He feigned an insulted look. "Roslyn, if I can examine a hissing, clawing cat, I think I can handle one sweet little baby."

She laughed. "Sorry. I'd forgotten you have that special touch."

Inside the bedroom, Chandler gently gathered Evelyn up from the bassinet and carried her across the hall to the nursery, where a changing table was positioned between the crib and a matching chest of drawers.

He was fastening the tabs on the clean diaper when

from the corner of his eye, he saw Roslyn step inside the door. Knowing she was watching his every move, he finished snapping the baby's onesie back together, then wrapped her in a light blanket.

He scooped up Evelyn from the changing table and cradled her safely in the crook of his left arm. "See, not so much as a tiny whimper," he playfully bragged.

"Where did you learn how to handle a baby?" she asked. "And don't tell me at the animal hospital. There is a huge difference between animal and human babies."

"To be honest, I learned a little about baby care way back when Vivian gave birth to Hannah. Viv was terrified she was going to do something wrong."

"That surprises me about Vivian. The night she visited the ranch, she came across as a very confident woman to me."

"She is now. But years ago when that jerk of an ex-husband left the ranch like a scalded hound, it shattered Viv's self-confidence. Not only about caring for the baby, but about everything. Holt and I and Joseph all helped her with the baby as much as we could. Until she finally woke up and realized she wasn't helpless, she was just divorced."

"Hannah is thirteen now. That was a long time ago," Roslyn stated. "Obviously you've not forgotten how to change a diaper."

He grinned. "You know what they say. Once you ride a bike you never forget. Same with dirty diapers."

Laughing, she moved out of the doorway. "Let's go to the living room," she suggested. "I've made coffee to go with the Italian cream cake you brought."

"That means I'll have to put Evelyn down," he complained.

"She can lie on the cushion next to you on the couch," Roslyn suggested.

"That's not the same as holding her."

Roslyn playfully rolled her eyes. "If you keep this up you're going to spoil her."

Wasn't that what fathers were for? Chandler caught himself before he said the question out loud. He wasn't Evelyn's father. But he felt like he was and everything inside of him wanted to be. Yet to say something like that would imply a serious commitment. Was he really ready to do that? To expose his heart?

Well, hell, Chandler. What are you doing here? It's not like you needed to leave the clinic and come over here to see Roslyn just to have something to do. When you left the office earlier, Trey and Cybil were still dealing with patients. But they'd insisted they could handle things because even they can see you've fallen in love with Roslyn and need to be with her. Don't you think it's time you face up to the reality that she already owns your heart?

Clearing his throat, he said, "Evelyn isn't going to be a spoiled little girl. She's going to be loved and protected."

The baby's warm weight against his chest was a feeling like nothing else he'd experienced and as he bent and kissed the top of her little head, he suddenly realized why his brothers were so happy. Joe and Blake had everything a man really needed.

By the time they finished dessert, Chandler had related everything that had been going on at the clinic and the ranch since he'd last seen her. Just hearing him talk about both places made Roslyn homesick, but she did her best not to show it.

Above anything, she needed to show him that moving here to town hadn't been a mistake. Her father had raised her to be a sponge and to Roslyn that was unacceptable. Yet at times, when she was feeling lonely and isolated, she wondered if she'd carried the independent thing a bit too far. Had living with the Hollisters really been that much of a crutch for her?

Staying there as an excuse to be close to Chandler was wrong, she firmly told herself. Especially if he had no plans to take their relationship a step further.

"Evelyn has fallen asleep again," he said as he smoothed a finger over the baby's fine hair. "Maybe I should put her back in her bed."

He was so incredibly gentle with Evelyn. Just watching the way he cradled the baby in his arms, the way he hummed and talked to her, filled Roslyn with bittersweet emotions. Would her daughter ever have a father who loved her as much as Chandler seemed to love her?

Not wanting to dwell on that melancholy question, Roslyn rose from the armchair. "Okay. While you do that I'll clean up our dinner mess."

Moments later, she placed the last dish in the dishwasher and closed the door just as Chandler entered the kitchen.

"She's sound asleep," he announced. "Do you need any help in here?"

"No. All finished."

Awkward silence suddenly filled the room and Roslyn watched him jam his hands in the front pockets of his jeans and lean a shoulder against the doorjamb.

"Is something wrong?" she asked.

"No. I'm just wondering what it's like for you living here—with just you and Evelyn."

She shrugged and walked over to him. "I've already told you that I like it. The apartment is cozy and convenient and has all the space the two of us need."

His eyes narrowed as he studied her face. “That’s not what I mean.”

“If you mean, do I get lonely, I’d be lying if I said I didn’t. After living at Three Rivers with lots of people around and things always happening, this little apartment is very quiet. But staying here is good for me,” she reasoned.

“Your voice is wobbling, Roslyn. If it’s so good for you, then why are you about to cry?”

Because she was feeling totally helpless, she thought. Because she was standing here looking at a man whom she loved with all her heart and he didn’t love her back. And probably never would.

“I’m not about to cry,” she lied. “I just get a little emotional when I talk about Three Rivers. While I was living there the ranch became very special to me.”

And that was definitely no lie, she thought. No matter what happened with Chandler in the future, she would never forget the beautiful ranch or the Hollister family.

His nostrils flared slightly as he pushed away from the door frame. “I was hoping I had become special to you,” he said quietly.

She wasn’t expecting anything like that to come out of his mouth, and for a moment, she could merely stare at him and wonder what was going on behind those blue, blue eyes.

“You are,” she admitted.

He moved close enough to wrap both his hands around her upper arms. Roslyn’s heart began to pound with anticipation.

“That’s hard to believe. I asked you to stay on the ranch. You refused.”

Was that disappointment she spotted in his eyes, or simply frustration?

Shaking her head, she said, "I explained to you that I needed to stand on my own for a while. And why are you bringing this up tonight? It's not like we haven't hashed it out before I left the ranch."

He moved his hands to her back and drew her forward until the front of her body was touching his. "No. We didn't hash it out. Not completely. Because at that time I didn't…no, I couldn't tell you how I really felt."

She flattened her palms against his chest and savored the warmth of his hard muscles. "Why not? I was there for over two weeks after Evelyn was born. You had plenty of opportunities to talk—about whatever it was that you wanted to tell me."

The sound he made in his throat was something between a cough and a groan.

"Yeah, I could talk. But I couldn't do this." Drawing her closer, he nuzzled his lips against her ear. "I couldn't show you how much I want you. How much I've been aching to make love to you."

Just hearing him speak the words was enough to turn her knees to mush. The sensation caused her fingers to instinctively clutch folds of his shirt to support herself.

"You couldn't? Why?"

Her voice was slurred with desire as she tilted her head and exposed the column of her neck to the searching warmth of his lips.

His arms tightened around her. "You'd just given birth," he reasoned. "And I wanted to give you time."

She slid her hands upward to his shoulders and gripped them tightly. "You should have told me how you felt, Chandler."

Delving his fingers into her hair, he turned her face until their gazes melded and only a scant space separated their lips. The connection stole her breath and scattered her senses in all directions.

"Would it have made any difference?" he asked.

The helpless moan in her throat was more like a sob. "Yes! Just to know that I was important to you in some way would've been—"

"You're important to me in *every* way, Ros. If I didn't realize that when you were at the ranch, I do now."

He wasn't exactly saying "I love you," but at this point, he was saying enough.

"Oh, Chandler."

Bringing her hands up to his face, she began to rain kisses over both his cheeks, his chin and finally the corners of his lips.

With a needy growl, he fastened his lips over hers and kissed her so deeply and passionately that she was instantly and totally lost to him.

The fiery contact went on and on, until her lungs were crying for air and her body was aching to connect to his. When he finally lifted his head and gazed down at her, his breathing was hard, his eyelids heavy.

"As much as I want you, this can't go on," he whispered gruffly. "Otherwise, I won't be able to stop. And I don't want to hurt you."

Before she could reply, he turned and walked a few steps away from her. Confused, she stared at his back.

"Hurt me? Why—?" Suddenly it dawned on her and she closed the space between them and rested a hand against his back. "Chandler, I promise, you're not going to hurt me."

"I can't take that chance. I—"

"No," she interrupted. "Listen, I just had my post-birth checkup yesterday. The doctor says I'm in great shape—if I feel like being intimate it will be fine."

Still uncertain, he turned back to her. "What about birth control? You're breastfeeding—" He suddenly paused and shook his head. "I'm sorry, Roslyn, I sound like a doctor. When I should be talking to you like a—"

"Lover?" she asked.

"Yes," he said sheepishly.

Smiling coyly, she moved forward until her breasts were pressing against his chest and her hips were aligned to his. "You need to quit worrying, Doc. The birth-control issue was taken care of while I was still in the hospital."

A horrified look came over his face. "You didn't do anything permanent, did you?"

Chuckling, she hugged him tighter. "No. Later on I'm going to want Evelyn to have brothers and sisters. When that time comes I can have the birth control removed."

He let out a relieved breath. "Oh. I'm glad I—" His arms came around her as he buried his face in the side of her hair. "I'm acting like an idiot, Ros. But nothing about my life has been the same since you left Three Rivers. I've missed you so much. I want you…more than you could possibly know."

She eased out of his arms and reached for his hand. "Maybe as much as I've been wanting you."

Not bothering to say more, she led him back to the bedroom and over to the queen-size bed covered with a fluffy red-and-white comforter.

Chandler looked over his shoulder at the bassinet. "What about Evelyn?"

Smiling impishly, Roslyn said, "She'll never know we're in here. But if it will make you feel better, I'll move her to the far side of the room."

She left him long enough to roll the bassinet to the opposite corner of the room, then returned to his side.

Chandler promptly gathered her up in his arms and gently laid her in the middle of the bed.

Laughing softly, she said, "Don't you think I'm wearing too many clothes for bed?"

"I'm going to take care of that problem in due time," he promised.

Her heart was pounding with eager anticipation as she watched him quickly discard his boots, then strip down to nothing but a pair of black boxers.

His body was everything she'd imagined it to be. Starting with his arms and ending with his legs, he was all hard, sculpted muscle and golden-brown skin. She couldn't wait to touch him and discover how it would feel to have her body tangled with his.

He climbed onto the bed and, kneeling over her, began to unbutton her blouse. Once the two pieces of fabric fell away and exposed her bra, his fingers traced the lacy edge, then cupped around the fullness of her breasts.

"I'm not exactly looking my best," she murmured. "I still have a bit of weight to lose and my skin is marked in places."

Smiling, his fingers lingered on her breasts for a few moments longer, then slipped downward over her midriff and onto the zipper of her jeans. "You couldn't look more beautiful to me than you do at this moment."

"You don't have to say that sort of thing to make me happy, Chandler. It's enough that you want me…like this."

By now he was tugging her jeans over her bare feet. Once he'd tossed them to the floor, she raised up so he could remove her blouse. When it was out of the way, he eased her back to the mattress, then stretched out next to her.

"Do you think I'm just mouthing words?" he asked as he pulled her into the circle of his arms.

Giddy with desire, Roslyn wrapped her arms around his neck. "I don't know what you're thinking," she admitted.

"Then it's time I showed you."

His lips found hers and as he kissed her hungrily, his hands reached to her back and unclasped her bra. When he peeled the fabric away, his fingers traced the outline of each breast and then his mouth left hers to brush against the soft sensitive skin.

The teasing sensation caused the aching need in her to build and spread, until she was certain it was going to consume her.

Then just when she was sure he was going to take one of the budded nipples into his mouth, his head lifted and he reclaimed her lips with another heated kiss.

By the time his tongue invited hers to mate with his, the room was spinning and every inch of her was burning with a need so intense she thought her body would ignite into a thousand tiny flames.

The taste of his mouth was a delicious mystery that made her want more and more, while the hard warmth of his body lured her senses to a place she'd never been before. Somewhere along the way, she realized she was crushed so tightly in his arms, she could scarcely move, much less breathe. But it didn't matter. Nothing mattered except making love to him.

When he finally eased himself off the bed and removed the last of their clothing, Roslyn had to bite back the needy whimpers clawing at the back of her throat.

Back on the bed, he positioned himself over her, but instead of connecting their bodies, he looked down at her and his blue eyes gently searched her face.

"Ros, are you sure about this—about me?"

His voice was thick with desire and yet she could also

hear something else. Something that sounded incredibly like love. Was that possible?

No. She wasn't going to think about that now. Tonight was all about giving him what he wanted and taking everything she needed.

Reaching up, she cradled his face with her hands. "I'm sure, Chandler. Very sure."

He let out a long breath and then with his eyes locked on her face, he parted her thighs and lowered his body down to hers.

Roslyn had thought she was prepared for him, but she'd been wrong. The sensation of having him inside her was like a thousand cymbals crashing together in her head. It sucked the oxygen from her lungs and rocked her equilibrium.

With a helpless groan, her fingers latched onto his shoulders. "Chandler. Oh, Chandler."

Lowering his face to hers, he kissed her forehead, her cheeks and finally her lips. "I know, my darling. It's too good. Too good."

Yes, it was too good, she thought. Because now, after this, after him, nothing was going to be the same.

The thought very nearly caused her to sob, but she swallowed the urge and pleaded, "Love me, Chandler. Please love me."

He answered her imploring request, and in a matter of moments Roslyn was meeting his rapid thrusts with a fierceness that stunned her.

Long minutes later, Chandler stared at the shadowy wall of the bedroom and wondered what had just happened to him. Taking Roslyn to bed had been like walking into a tornado and he was still shaking from the aftermath.

From the very first night Roslyn had come into his life, he'd recognized that she was different from the women he'd dated in the past. He'd not understood exactly why she'd evoked such tender feelings in him, but she had. And because of her situation with the baby and her father, he'd tried his best to tamp down his emotions and think of her simply as a woman in need. But that hadn't worked. Now, more than two months had passed and he could no longer deny that he loved her utterly. But would the future take her and the baby away from him?

The soft touch of her hands against his back tugged his thoughts to the present and he rolled over so that his face was next to hers on the pillow.

"Is something wrong, Chandler?"

His hand trembling, he smoothed strands of tangled brown hair from her face and tried to give her an easy smile.

"Nothing is wrong, my sweet. I'm just trying to get my wind back." He rested his forehead against hers. "Besides, I'm the one who should be asking if you're okay."

She curved her arm around his waist and drew the front of her damp body next to his. The feel of her full breasts and soft thighs brushing against him made his loins ache to have her again. It was crazy how much he wanted her. How much he figured he would always want her.

"Mmm. I'm more than okay. I feel—"

He pulled his head back to see uncertainty swimming in her eyes. "You feel what?" he prompted. "Do you wish this hadn't happened?"

"Oh, no, Chandler. I'm not thinking anything like that." She touched her fingertips to the indentation in his chin. "I was just trying to decide how to tell you that… I love you."

He went stock-still and for a moment he thought his heart had quit beating. "Love…me," he said. "Roslyn, what just happened with us, it…was incredible, but—"

Her gaze dropped from his face and she pulled slightly back from him. "You don't have to explain or make excuses. Just because I love you doesn't mean I expect you to automatically feel the same about me. But I decided—" Sighing, she rolled to her back and stared at the ceiling. "After the huge mistake I made with Erich, I don't want anything hidden between you and me."

Propping himself up on one elbow, he gazed down at her soft features. "I don't want anything hidden, either," he said gently. "And if you hadn't stopped me a moment ago, you would've heard me say how much I love you, too."

Her gaze fluttered warily up to his face and she stared at him in stunned disbelief. "You…love me? Chandler, I—"

He waited for her to finish, but no words followed. Instead, a trail of tears slipped down her cheeks.

"Roslyn, why are you crying? What's wrong?"

Her head twisted back and forth on the pillow. "Because…this all has to be a dream. I'm afraid I'm going to wake up and you'll be gone."

Was she really that insecure? Couldn't she see how much he adored her?

"Oh, darling Ros, why would you think that? I'm here. And I have no intentions of leaving or letting you slip away."

Her brown eyes were still wet with tears and filled with doubt. "You already have a wonderful life, Chandler. A huge, loving family. A thriving business. Devoted friends. You don't need me and Evelyn. Especially when you can have any woman."

Groaning, he reached to pull her close. “Even if I could have any woman, I don’t want her. I want you.”

“I don’t know why. I’m just a runaway with too much baggage and too many scars. My father tells me I need to grow up or I’ll never be able to hold a man.”

Wrapping his arms tightly around her, he said, “I think the man needs to work on his own problems before he gives out advice. But we’ll discuss him later. Right now I don’t want to waste this night with talk. Do you?”

She smiled at him and his heart swelled as he wiped at the track of tears on her face.

“No,” she whispered. “I don’t want to waste a moment.”

He lowered his lips to hers and as he kissed her, he recognized, for the first time in his life, he was tasting real love.

Chapter Twelve

The next morning, Hollister Animal Hospital was overrun with patients, and to make matters worse Cybil was late getting to work because she'd been helping her sister tow her dead car to a garage to be repaired.

He hadn't fully expected to be finished with everyone on the appointment book, plus a few walk-ins, by the time lunch hour rolled around. But somehow he and the staff had cleared the place. Since he rarely left the building, other than to make a house call, Loretta had looked surprised when he'd told her he was going downtown and wouldn't be back until the clinic reopened at one.

Chandler hadn't told any of the staff where he was going. His plans were too private and special to share with anyone, except the woman he loved.

A few minutes later, when he walked up on the small porch of Roslyn's apartment, he could hear Evelyn screaming angrily. But by the time Roslyn opened the door to greet him, the baby had quieted to intermittent howls.

In spite of the noise, Roslyn didn't appear to be the least bit flustered. In fact, the smile on her face had to be the warmest, most inviting one he'd ever seen.

"Chandler! Come in before Evelyn disturbs the whole neighborhood!" She reached for his hand and tugged him over the threshold.

Chandler stepped past Roslyn and into the foyer. "She must be wanting her lunch."

Roslyn shook her head. "She's already had lunch. She's angry because I took her out of the bathtub and dressed her."

Chandler laughed. "So she's already a little diva and doesn't want her bubble bath to be interrupted. What a girl!"

"'What a girl' is right," Roslyn said with a chuckle. "I can already see her teenage years ahead. I'm not expecting them to be easy."

She raised up on her tiptoes and lifted her face to receive his kiss. The sweet contact of having his lips on hers brought the night before rushing back to him, and from the wash of pink on her cheeks, he figured she was remembering, too.

"This is a wonderful surprise," she murmured. "How did you manage to get away from the clinic at this time of day?"

"It must be the full moon," he said jokingly. "All my patients were cooperative this morning."

She linked her arm through his and urged him on to the living room. "Have you eaten yet? I'll fix you a sandwich and iced tea."

"I...don't have time to eat. I need to be back at the clinic by one. And I want to talk with you."

Both her brows arched coyly. "Just talk?"

Grinning, he pulled her close and placed a long kiss on her lips. "Yes, just talk for now. But later tonight might be different," he suggested.

"I'll take that as a promise." She gestured to the couch. "Grab a seat and I'll put Evelyn in her crib. I think she's beginning to see the mobile. That might keep her occupied."

Normally he would've ignored her offer to take a seat and followed her to the nursery so he could hold Evelyn. But with the few minutes he had quickly ticking away, he didn't want to get sidetracked.

"All right," he told her. "I'll wait right here."

While she was gone, he double-checked his pocket and sighed with relief as his fingers came into contact with the small, fabric-covered box. Damn it, he should've taken the time to stop and buy flowers, too. But those would have to come later tonight, he thought, when he took her to Jose's for dinner.

"Wonder of wonders," Roslyn said as she reentered the living room. "As soon as I put her in the crib, the crying stopped and her eyelids drooped. She's probably already asleep."

"I'm glad. Because I need your undivided attention."

He patted the cushion next to his and she obliged by sinking down close to his side.

"Okay, so what is this about? Returning to work at the clinic?"

He looked at her with surprise. "Why would you think that? Evelyn isn't two months old yet and I know you want to spend as much time with her as possible."

She shrugged. "I've been talking with Loretta. She says Cybil is running herself ragged and causing extra work for you. It's obvious you could use my help."

"Would you like to work at the clinic again? I mean, later on, after Evelyn gets a little older."

She reached for his hand and rubbed her fingertips over the back of it. Her touch helped soothe the anxious beat of his heart.

"I loved working at the clinic," she said. "But whether I go back later depends on how you feel about it."

He took a deep breath and let it out. "That's what I wanted to talk with you about—to tell you exactly what I want. For you and me and Evelyn."

Her lips parted as her gaze searched his face. "What are you saying, Chandler? Are you asking me to move back to Three Rivers?"

He clasped both her hands between his. "Yes, I am. I asking you to come back to Three Rivers as my wife."

"Wife."

She repeated the word as though she'd never heard it before and Chandler could see he'd shocked her.

"That's right. I want you to be my wife, Roslyn. I want Evelyn to be my daughter." Rather than wait for her to reply, he reached to his shirt pocket. As he pulled out the box and flipped open the lid, her brown eyes grew wider and wider. "Will you marry me, Roslyn DuBose?"

Shaking her head, she let out a sound that was something between a laugh and a sob. "I don't understand, Chandler. When did you decide this?"

"Probably when I carried you into the clinic that first night we met."

She groaned. "Be serious, Chandler."

"I am being serious. I wanted to wrap my arms around you and never let go. I still feel that way. I'll always feel that way." He took the ring from its velvet bed and pushed it onto the appropriate finger. "If you don't like the ring, you can change it for something else. And it might need to be resized. I guessed at the fit."

She gazed down at the large, emerald cut diamond flanked by two smaller round diamonds.

"It's unbelievably beautiful, Chandler. And the size is perfect. But I—" She looked at him and shook her head. "Are you truly certain this is what you want? Last night—"

"I've been thinking about this long before last night, Roslyn. I love you. I love Evelyn. You're everything I want. All I need now is for you to say yes."

She looked at the ring, then back up to his eager face. "I love you so much, Chandler. The only thing I can say is yes. Yes! Yes!"

Flinging her arms around him, she pressed her lips to his and as he kissed her, Chandler felt as if everything in the world had righted itself.

When their lips finally parted, he pressed his cheek against hers and held her tight against him. "I know you're probably wondering about my work and how I'll ever make time for you and the baby. But I will. I promise I'll make it happen. We're going to be happy—together."

She pulled her head back far enough to look at him and the joy he saw in her eyes made his spirits soar even higher.

"I'm not worried. Blake and Joe have managed to balance work and marriage. Whatever your brothers can do, you can do, too."

"Dang right," he said with a chuckle. "Now, when are we going to set the date? I'm sure you'll want enough time to plan a wedding and that's okay with me. As long as you make it quick."

Laughing, she squeezed his hands. "You mean, like a few-days quick? Or a few-weeks quick?"

"I'm thinking days, but I want you to be happy. Maybe with Mom and Vivian and Katherine and Tessa all helping with wedding plans, you can shave the wedding date down to a month from now."

She leaned forward and kissed him again. "Oh, Chandler, I don't need a fancy wedding. As far as I'm concerned I'd be happy to elope to Reno or somewhere. But then I'd feel badly about knocking your family out of the celebration. Maybe we can compromise with a simple ceremony on the ranch?"

He nodded. "That sounds perfect. Because I wouldn't feel good about leaving out family, either. And Roslyn, speaking of family—I really want you to contact your father and let him know about the baby, and me, and the wedding. It would be the right thing to do."

Like the flip of a light switch, her expression suddenly turned incredulous.

"You expect me to contact my father? After all I've told you? I can't believe I'm hearing you right, Chandler!"

Pulling her hands from his, she rose from the couch and walked across the room. Chandler stared after her. He'd expected her to be resistant to the idea, but not this vehemently.

"I don't think my suggestion is that outrageous, Roslyn," he reasoned. "This is an eventful time in your life. I'm thinking you should want to show your father that you're happy. That you're now the mother of a beautiful daughter and a wife to me."

She turned around and even at a distance he could see the anguish twisting her features. "I'm not inhuman, Chandler. It would give me great satisfaction to show him how much he misjudged me. I'd like for him to see I'm a capable person and can stand on my own without him dictating my every move. Trouble is, his interfering wouldn't stop there, Chandler. You see, happiness doesn't factor in to Martin DuBose's plans. Whether my mother or I was ever happy has never been his concern. He's only interested in having things his way. To put it bluntly, he'd cause us all kinds of hell."

Chandler left the couch and walked over to where she stood. Her hands were clenched and her breathing was coming in short bursts. The sight of her anger was contagious and in spite of his normally cool head, he was rapidly losing his patience.

"What exactly do you think I am, Roslyn? Just a bystander? A milksop who's afraid to come out of the shadows and defend the woman he loves?"

Confused, she stared at him. "No. Of course I don't think that. But—"

"There are no buts, Roslyn," he interrupted. "If I'm going to be your husband, then all of this affects me, too. Your problems become mine and vice versa. No matter what they are, we need to resolve them together. And the way I see it, you can't expect to move happily into the future until you resolve this thing with your father. My Lord, Ros, the man doesn't even know where you are!"

"And I'm better off for it!"

She practically yelled the words at him and as Chandler studied the fury on her face, disappointment welled up in him until he was practically choking on it.

"I can see this isn't going to work," he said dully.

"You're darn right it isn't going to work!" She stalked past him and didn't stop until she'd put a measurable distance between them. "I just got out from under one man's thumb. I don't intend to turn around and tie myself to another. Not a man who wants to dictate my life before I even become his wife! No! This isn't going to work for me."

The day had started like a beautiful fairy tale, Chandler thought. The sky had never been a more vivid blue and the breeze was as fresh as a spring flower. He was blessed with a job he loved and, even more importantly, the woman he'd prayed would come into his life and fill it with happiness.

Fairy tales aren't real, Chandler. And apparently the love Roslyn professed to feel for you wasn't real, either.

Chandler was sure something inside him was dying, yet somehow he managed to close the space between them. Her lovely features were defiant and so far removed from the woman he'd proposed to only minutes ago, that he felt he was looking at a stranger.

"There for a moment, I was beginning to question myself. I was wondering if I might be wrong and you were right. But that hardly matters now. You've just shown me that your father is the smart one in all of this. You're not mature enough to be a wife to me or any man."

She opened her mouth to make a retort, but Chandler didn't bother to stand there and listen. She'd already made it very clear how she felt.

As he started out of the room, she yelled at him, "Here. You can take your diamond and your oh-so-perfect ideas with you."

Chandler felt the ring hit his back and heard the ping as the piece of jewelry fell on the hardwood floor. The sound was like a gavel at the end of a trial, he decided. Everything had reached a conclusion and it wasn't a happy one.

"I don't want it," he said without a backward glance. "Keep it and add it to your collection."

Roslyn was in the kitchen, packing items into heavy-duty cardboard boxes, when the doorbell rang.

Wiping her hands on the seat of her jeans, she walked out to the foyer and wondered what she would do if the person on the other side of the door was Chandler. Which was a moot question altogether. More than a week had passed since Chandler had proposed marriage, then turned around and walked out of her life. No. He'd be the last person to be standing on the porch of her apartment.

To her relief the caller was Katherine and she quickly opened the door wide and invited her inside.

"This is a wonderful surprise," Roslyn told her. "Are you just getting off work?"

Katherine nodded. "I thought I'd pop by and say hello before I drove on home to the ranch. How's little Evelyn?"

"She's asleep in the nursery. Go take a peep at her while I make us some coffee," Roslyn told her.

Moments later, as Roslyn poured water into the coffee machine, Katherine entered the kitchen, then stopped and stared at the partially filled boxes.

"What in the world? Surely you're not sending these things to charity. It all looks new to me."

Roslyn bit down on her lip. "No. Not to charity. I'm getting it organized. Before I call a moving van."

Katherine made her way through the boxes on the floor to join Roslyn at the cabinet counter.

"Moving van! Have you found a different apartment already?"

Roslyn couldn't bring herself to look at Katherine. During her stay at Three Rivers, the woman had become like a sister to her. "No. I'm…leaving Wickenburg. I've decided it's time I move on to Redding and settle down on Mother's property."

"Oh. Gosh, I don't know what to say. Except that I wish you wouldn't go. Everyone here loves you so much. And actually…well, I'm not supposed to say anything, but given the circumstances, I think I'd better. Maureen has been very busy putting a baby shower together for you. I think she's planned it for next Saturday night at the ranch. She wanted to surprise you."

Maureen didn't have time to draw a deep breath much less plan a shower for Roslyn—a party that she didn't deserve. Especially now that everything had ended between her and Chandler.

Suddenly the anguish in her heart was too much to hold back and she pressed her hands over her face to hide her tears. "Oh, God, Katherine, this is terrible. Just terrible."

Taking her by the shoulders, Katherine led her over to the kitchen table and eased her into the nearest chair. "Roslyn, what's happened? Tell me."

Choking back her sobs, Roslyn related everything that had happened, starting with Chandler proposing, the engagement ring and ultimately the quarrel over her father.

"I ruined everything, Kat. But I didn't see that I had much choice. If I invited Dad back into my life, he'd make sure everything would be ruined, anyway. So Chandler put me in a no-win situation."

Katherine went to the cabinet and filled two cups with the freshly brewed coffee. After spooning powdered creamer into both, she carried them over to the table.

"Drink. It'll make you feel better."

"Thanks, Katherine," she said ruefully. "I'm surprised you still want to stay and have coffee with me. Now that you've heard the whole story. And you know that I've… well, probably hurt Chandler."

Shaking her head, Katherine said, "Don't be silly. Besides, I can see how all of this has hurt you, too. Frankly, I'm stunned. Chandler hasn't spoken a word of this to Blake or Holt. They would've already said something.

And Maureen certainly doesn't know. She's still planning the party as though nothing is wrong."

This news only caused more tears to sprout from Roslyn's eyes. "This is awful. Truly awful. I'll have to tell her. I can't go out to the ranch. Not now. Besides, Maureen is going to hate me once she hears what happened. And Chandler—I couldn't face him. Not for any reason."

"Maureen isn't going to hate you. But I can tell you this, she's going to be terribly angry if you up and leave Wickenburg like this."

Roslyn reached for the coffee and took several sips and tried to gather her composure. "I don't really see any point of staying here, Katherine. Yes, I love it here and, yes, I've made lots of great friends on the ranch and at the animal hospital. But being here—I couldn't forget Chandler."

"Is that what you really want? To forget him? You told me a few minutes ago that you love him."

"I do! I guess I always will. But he sees everything differently than me." She paused and sucked in a painful breath. "I don't think he ever understood the cold expanse between me and my father. Or the heartache I've endured because of him. If he had understood, he wouldn't have asked me to include him in my plans…our plans."

Smiling gently, Katherine reached over and patted Roslyn's hand. "Chandler probably doesn't understand you completely. But on the other hand, I don't believe you understand him, either."

Gripping her coffee cup, she looked at the other woman. "What do you mean?"

"Chandler is a born nurturer. He wants everything and everyone, human or animal, to be well and happy. There's not a vindictive or spiteful bone in his body. In fact, his brothers often complain that he's too laid-back and too easy with people that he should get angry with."

"He certainly got angry with me." The icy fury Roslyn had spotted in his eyes just before he'd walked away was something she'd never forget.

"Yes, he can get angry. But mostly he's a caring guy. And, in many ways, I think the death of his father was even worse on him than his brothers."

Surprised by the remark, Roslyn asked, "Why would you think that? I'm sure each of them was equally devastated."

"Yes. But Chandler carries the extra burden of resembling his late father and having the man's gentle personality. Everyone, even Maureen, expects him to always be like Joel."

"That's too much to expect from Chandler," Roslyn murmured. "Just like it was too much for him to expect me to throw my arms open to my father."

"You might be right. But Chandler has no father now. And I'm sure he'd tell you that he doesn't want that same emptiness for you. He wants every aspect of your life to be full and happy. That's just the kind of guy he is. A nurturer," she repeated.

"So you're trying to tell me that you think I'm wrong."

Shaking her head, Katherine reached for her coffee. "It's not my place to tell you what's right or wrong, Ros. But if you love Chandler, you shouldn't be running away."

"I'm afraid, Kat." Rising to her feet, she began to wander restlessly around the kitchen. "And though it probably doesn't look like it to you, I love Chandler too much to drag him into a family that was...never really much of a family. He deserves better. He deserves a father-in-law who would embrace him instead of reject him."

Katherine's cynical laugh brought Roslyn's pacing to

a halt and she looked over to the table to see a wry twist on her friend's face.

"Oh, Roslyn, when Blake and I fell in love I had all kinds of awful baggage. My first marriage was a disaster and I blamed myself for my husband's death. And Dad…well, I harbored plenty of bitter memories toward him. After he became disabled with a stroke, I questioned whether I was doing the right thing to move back to Wickenburg to care for him. But in spite of my misgivings, Nick and I moved back in with him."

Roslyn had to ask, "How did that go?"

A sad smile touched her face. "We had a little over two good years with him before he passed away. I didn't think I would be devastated over his death. He'd caused my mother and brother and me so much sorrow and humiliation. But I was devastated to lose him. And later, after I'd had time to think about everything, I regretted that I stayed away from Dad all those years. Because I realized that in helping my father, I was also helping myself."

More tears began to stream from Roslyn's eyes. "I'm not sure I'm capable of helping my father change. But I suppose it's never too late to try, is it?"

The somber expression on Katherine's face suddenly turned into a bright smile. "Never," she agreed. Then she jumped to her feet and carried one of the cardboard boxes over to the cabinet counter.

When she started pulling out the contents, Roslyn asked blankly, "What are you doing?"

"Unpacking. So hurry up and let's get this stuff back where it belongs before Evelyn wakes up."

Two days later, hours after the clinic had closed for the night, Chandler and Trey were still working at the barn.

"Is his leg mending, Doc? I sure hope so. His horns are as big as baseball bats. I want him to go home. Pronto."

Chandler made a thorough inspection of the stitches he'd sewn into the bull's back leg. "The laceration is healing. If he doesn't develop a fever I'll send him home tomorrow. Have you given him the shot of antibiotics?"

"Yep. All done."

"Good." Chandler motioned for Trey to move aside, then opened the squeeze chute to allow the black bull to move into the holding pen.

Without bothering to look back, Trey rushed past Chandler and out the nearest gate. "Better run, Doc! He's mad as hell!"

Unconcerned, Chandler walked through the gate Trey had just rushed through. Behind him, the bull had already turned his attention to a pile of alfalfa in the hay manger.

"He's not mad. He's hungry." Chandler secured the lock on the gate, then glanced over to where Trey was washing the manure off his boots with a garden hose. "How about me and you changing clothes and driving over to the Fandango? It's Friday night. The place will be hopping."

Dropping the hose, the lanky blond turned a disbelieving stare at Chandler.

"Doc, are you feeling okay?"

Grimacing, Chandler lifted the hat from his head and raked a hand through his hair. Actually, he felt like he'd been run over by a herd of stampeding cattle. But he needed something to blot out the miserable thoughts going on in his head.

"Hell yes, I feel okay. Why are you looking at me like I'm crazy? It might do us both good to have a few drinks and do a little dancing."

"Who are we going to dance with?" As soon as Trey

had asked the question, he laughed. "Dumb question, huh? Women take one look at you and it's all over for me."

As the two men began walking down the sloping ground to the back entrance of the clinic, Chandler said, "What are you talking about? You're the Romeo of Yavapai County."

Trey laughed. "Sure, Doc. Even if I was a Romeo I don't think going to the Fandango is a good idea."

Trey's negative response surprised Chandler. Normally the guy was always ready for any kind of entertainment. Especially a trip to the notorious nightclub.

"Why not?" he asked.

Groaning, Trey said, "I always end up getting into a fight. And I don't particularly like nursing a black eye."

Chandler said, "You wouldn't get a black eye if you'd lead with your left instead of your right."

"Oh, Doc, you don't know what I lead with," Trey complained. "And I don't believe for one minute that you really want to go to a honky-tonk. Yeah, it's Friday night, but we got to deal with that herd of goats over at the Tabor farm early in the morning."

"That'll be quick work."

Chandler opened the door and started down the hallway to his office. Trey clomped behind him.

"Sure," Trey said mockingly. "Three hours at the quickest. Besides, Roslyn wouldn't like it if she heard you were out carousing around."

The middle of Chandler's chest winced with pain. Nearly two weeks had passed since he'd walked out of Roslyn's apartment and, try as he might, he couldn't forget her or baby Evelyn. He couldn't push away the pain of losing them, much less look into the future. There was nothing there but a black, empty pit.

"What's Roslyn got to do with anything?" He picked up a stack of files on the corner of his desk, while cutting a glance at Trey. The other man appeared astounded by his question.

"Well, hell, Doc. She has everything to do with it. I thought you were crazy about her."

Dropping the files back to the desk, Chandler walked over and sank onto the couch where Roslyn had lain after her fainting spell. That night, like every other moment he'd spent with her, continued to roll through his head, reminding him that he was nothing more than a stupid fool.

"I don't really want to talk about Roslyn," he said bluntly. "She's moving on."

The crestfallen look on Trey's face made Chandler feel even worse, if that was possible.

"Dang. She told all of us here at the clinic that she wanted to come back to work after the baby got a little older. Did you tell her she couldn't work here anymore or something?"

Or something, Chandler thought sickly. "No. I didn't tell her that. We, uh, we just went our different ways, that's all."

"Well, you could knock me over with a feather. I got the feeling that the two of you were going to be permanent."

Chandler grunted cynically. "Trey, a man can't count on anything being permanent. Especially when it comes to a woman."

"Yeah," Trey mumbled in agreement. "Another good reason we shouldn't go to the Fandango."

"Hey, can't a guy get some service around here?"

Both men jerked their heads around to see Joseph sauntering through the door, and since his brother was wearing a deputy sheriff's uniform, Chandler figured he had to be ending his shift, or just beginning one.

"What's going on?" Chandler asked in the cheeriest voice he could muster. "Did you come to arrest us for bad behavior?"

Joseph chuckled. "Knowing you two, I should probably haul you in for lacking common sense."

"Nobody ever accused us of being geniuses, Joe," Trey joked. "'Course, Doc is pretty darned close to one."

Rolling his eyes at that, Chandler gestured to the empty end of the couch. "Have time to sit a minute?" he asked Joseph.

"No. I'm on my way home and I'm running late, as usual. I have something out in the truck for you. Better come get it."

The three men trooped outside to where Joseph's pickup truck was parked. When he opened the back door, Chandler immediately heard a cacophony of yips and whines.

"Is that what I think it is?" Chandler asked.

Joseph reached in and pulled out a black-and-white spotted pup, no more than three months old. He was scrawny and dirty and trembling with fright. Chandler's heart went as soft as a marshmallow.

"Where did you find him?"

"Take a guess. On the side of the road. Somebody didn't want him," Joseph said. "I told Connor you'd take him. You couldn't turn down a stray if your life depended on it."

Joseph handed the dog over to Chandler, who immediately turned around and handed the animal to Trey.

"You know what to do to take care of him," he told Trey. "The end kennel is empty. Put him in it."

"Right, Doc. I'll fix the little guy."

Trey left with the pup and Joseph shut the back door on the truck, then opened the driver's door and climbed into the vehicle.

Before he had had a chance to back away, Chandler asked, "How's Little Joe and Tessa?"

"Little Joe is just like his uncle Holt—he's turning into a mischievous rascal and he never shuts up." The grin on Joseph's face deepened. "Tessa's been throwing up. Don't tell anybody yet, but we think she's pregnant."

Pregnant. Another Hollister baby. For those few brief minutes Roslyn had worn his engagement ring, he'd believed Evelyn would be his child. Now some other man would eventually become her father. The idea left a sick, heavy feeling in his heart.

"Lucky you," he said with as much enthusiasm as he could summon.

"Yeah. Lucky me." His expression suddenly wistful, he looked at Chandler. "Tessa and I are truly blessed to have Little Joe and a baby on the way. But there's a bittersweetness about it, too. We can't help but wish our fathers, and Tessa's mother, were around to enjoy their grandkids. Mom is the only grandparent our children will have."

Chandler forced a smile. "Thank God for Mom. She'll be happy when you give her the news."

Joseph shut the door and put the truck into Reverse. Leaning his head out the open window, he said, "Gotta go, brother. Take care of that pup. I figure by the time Evelyn starts crawling, she'll need a furry playmate."

Lifting a hand in farewell, Joseph drove away. Chandler thoughtfully watched his brother's truck disappear into the darkness.

Their father, Joel, was gone. Tessa's father, Ray Maddox, had also died a few short months before she'd come to Arizona. And Katherine's father, Avery, passed away before he'd had a chance to see his daughter marry Blake and give birth to the twins.

It was too late for those men, Chandler thought. But Roslyn and her father could still have a worthwhile relationship, if they were willing to work at it. Still, that was something Roslyn needed to decide for herself, not because Chandler pushed her into it.

He'd been wrong to insist she contact her father. These past hellish weeks without her and Evelyn had taught him just how wrong. Instead of urging her to mend the broken bridges behind her, he should've been vowing his love and support. He should have been convincing her that she and the baby were the most important things in his life. Not her relationship with Martin DuBose.

But if Chandler went to her and admitted that he'd been stupid and wrong, would she be willing to forgive him? Would she give him another chance? He didn't know. He only knew he had to try. Otherwise, his chance at real happiness was going to be forever and truly over.

Chapter Thirteen

Early the next morning, after Chandler and Trey finished treating the goats and returned to the clinic, he changed into clean clothes and headed straight to Roslyn's apartment.

The sight of her Jaguar parked beneath the covered carport was a relief. At least she hadn't run away for a second time, he thought. But who was driving the black sedan parked directly behind Roslyn's Jag? The bar code on the license plate suggested it was a rental.

Had a friend come all the way from Fort Worth to visit? Or had Roslyn's father finally tracked her down?

He didn't care if he was interrupting. Roslyn was the woman he loved. He wasn't leaving until he'd talked with her and she understood how much he still wanted them to make a life together.

After parking the truck behind the sedan, Chandler hurried to the front porch and was about to punch the doorbell when he noticed the door was slightly ajar. What the hell was going on? Roslyn didn't leave her doors open.

He knocked on the doorjamb in hopes the sound would draw Roslyn's attention. After a few moments passed and she didn't appear, he decided to forgo manners. He entered the house and started down the short foyer toward the living room. Halfway there, he picked up on a man's voice. Low and gruff, it was as cold as a snow-capped mountain, and the sound caused Chandler to stop in his tracks.

"Do you have any idea of the embarrassment you've caused me, Roslyn? The shame you have brought on the DuBose name by your irresponsible behavior?"

As Chandler listened to the man's questions it was all he could do to keep from running into the room and knocking him flat on the floor. But he understood that Roslyn needed a chance to fight her battle with the man, before he stepped in to back her up.

She said, "I'm sorry that's how you see things, Dad. I called you, hoping the time I've been away might've softened your feelings. That you'd want to see me and your grandchild. But obviously I was hoping for too much."

"Soft. You can't get ahead in the world by being soft, Roslyn. And you would try to twist things around and make me look like the villain in all of this." The coldness in his voice turned to sarcasm. "Now I've got to try to explain to my friends and colleagues why my own daughter ran away from home. It's indecent. And I'm telling you one thing, when we get back to Fort Worth, you will do exactly as I say. Nothing more. Nothing less."

Chandler took a step forward with the intention of revealing his presence, but Roslyn began to speak and he forced himself to pause.

"You've misunderstood, Dad. I invited you out here because I thought as my father you had a right to see your granddaughter. But that's where it ends. I have no intention of going back to Fort Worth or living in the same house with you again."

The man let out a scoffing laugh. "And what do you think you're going to do? Are you thinking you'll take the money your mother left you and buy your own place? If so, I should remind you that I can find some sort of legal loophole to take every penny you have away from you."

"I suppose that would make you feel superior to take your granddaughter's financial security away from her," Roslyn said stiffly. "Well, go ahead. I honestly don't care what you do with any of the money. My life is here now. With the man I love. The man I'm going to marry. That's all that matters to me."

Joy flooded through Chandler, while Martin DuBose snorted loudly.

"Marry you? Who? Some blue-collar worker with a big heart and an empty bank account? I really think—"

Chandler had heard enough. He walked into the room and faced the man who was the reason Roslyn had run from Texas and straight into his arms.

Gasping with surprise, Roslyn stepped toward him. "Chandler! I…didn't hear the doorbell. Were you—?"

He moved to Roslyn's side and wrapped an arm around the back of her waist.

"The front door was open and no one answered so I came in, anyway," he explained. "I've been standing in the foyer."

Uncertainty pinched her features. "So you heard what was being said?"

He gazed down at her and hoped his eyes were conveying all the love he felt for her. "More than enough," he answered softly, then turned his attention to her father.

"I'm Dr. Chandler Hollister," he said, introducing himself to the tall, lean man with iron-gray hair. "And yes, I wear a blue collar. It's usually denim like the one I have on now. 'Cause it's tough as hell and hard to tear."

Suddenly uncomfortable, Martin DuBose cleared his throat. "Am I safe to assume you are my daughter's fiancé, Dr. Hollister?"

Roslyn reached for Chandler's hand and the sight of the emerald cut diamond on her finger told him everything he needed to know. She'd already forgiven him.

"I am."

"Chandler is a veterinarian," Roslyn said proudly. "He and his family own one of the largest ranches in the state of Arizona. But that's not why I'm marrying him. No, it's because he's the kindest, most hard-working and honorable man I've ever known. And I love him with all my heart."

For a moment her father appeared totally stunned by his daughter's statement. Then he straightened his shoulders and walked to the opposite side of the room. With his back to them, he stared out the picture window, but Chandler figured the man wasn't seeing anything except the empty life he'd created for himself.

After a moment, Martin said, "I see. So I guess you think you don't need me anymore."

Roslyn glance incredulously at Chandler before she replied to her father's comment. "I need a father who will love me even when I don't do the right or perfect thing."

Martin turned and the regret on his face proved to Chandler that Roslyn would eventually have the father she deserved. It might take months or even years for that to happen, but at least there was a chance.

Evelyn's loud cry suddenly broke the awkward silence and Chandler looked at Roslyn and smiled. "I'll go take care of our daughter. You and your father have plenty to talk about."

Epilogue

Roslyn peeked into the crib, then walked across the room to where Chandler was already settled between the covers of their queen-size bed.

"Our daughter was asleep before I got her pajamas on," she said.

Sliding next to her husband's side, she sighed with contentment as he switched off the bedside lamp and pillowed her head on his shoulder.

"I can't believe the ranch house is finally quiet," Chandler murmured against the top of her head.

Roslyn chuckled. "It was a great Halloween party. Evelyn worked hard to keep up with the twins and Little Joe."

At six months old, Evelyn had grown into a cheerful baby with big brown eyes, dimpled cheeks and a head full of light brown curls. Chandler adored their daughter and was already making noises to Roslyn about giving her a brother or sister.

He said, "Well, it won't be long before her crawl turns into a walk and then she'll really be able to chase after the big kids. If you ask me, Hannah and Nick had the best idea. They slipped upstairs with a bagful of candy and watched reruns of *The Munsters*."

"Just seeing those two cousins together makes me smile," Roslyn said. "It's so wonderful that Vivian and Sawyer are finally expecting a baby this spring. And with Tessa about to give birth any day now, we're going to have plenty to celebrate this Thanksgiving."

He nuzzled his nose against her temple. "Yes, the holidays are going to be very special this year. Hannah is finally going to get the sibling she's always wanted. Tessa and Joe are about to get their second child. And you and I are—"

"Happier than I ever thought possible," she finished dreamily.

Marrying Chandler five months ago and living here at Three Rivers had given her everything Roslyn had ever wanted. A loving, devoted husband and a home filled with a tight-knit family. Chandler's workload was still heavy, but he'd taken the step to lighten it by hiring another male assistant to help him and Trey handle the bigger jobs. And recently Roslyn had resumed working at the clinic on a part-time basis. Since the job gave her a chance to care for the animals, plus spend more time with her husband, it was a winning situation for everyone.

As for Roslyn's father, he'd relented somewhat and attended her and Chandler's wedding, which had been a beautiful outdoor ceremony on the front lawn of the ranch. Since then, her father had visited Three Rivers twice and though things were hardly perfect between him and Roslyn, they were slowly changing for the better.

Chandler's fingers gently turned her face toward his and the moonlight filtering through the windows illuminated the provocative grin on his face. "I was about to say you and I are going to add to our little family, God willing."

She whispered, "I have a feeling that our little family is going to turn into a big one."

As his fingers traced gentle circles on her bare shoulder, he went suddenly quiet and Roslyn glanced up at his pensive expression.

"What are you thinking?" she asked. "Are you worried I can't deal with more than one child?"

"Not at all. You're a wonderful mother, sweetheart. You could tie one hand behind your back and easily deal with six more babies. To be honest, I was thinking about Mom and all these new grandbabies she's getting. On the surface she acts like she's on top of the world. But when she believes we're not looking...well, I'm more certain than ever that she's hiding something from us."

His comment prompted Roslyn to lever herself up on one elbow and gaze down at him. "I haven't mentioned this, Chandler, because I didn't want to worry you needlessly, but the other day I went to Maureen's office to give her a message from Reeva and found her with tears on her face."

Frowning, he asked, "Mom was crying? Was she on the phone?"

"She wasn't doing anything, just staring out the window. Which is totally unlike her. I asked her what was wrong and she passed it off as nothing more than a blue mood. Chandler, did Holt or Joe tell her about those items they found? The piece of shirt fabric and the belt tip?"

He shook his head. "None of us have breathed a word about it. Joe has them locked away. No, I think something else is going on with her."

"Like what?"

A few silent seconds ticked by and then he answered,

"A man. I don't know if it's Uncle Gil or someone else, but I think Mom has fallen in love and doesn't want us to know that she's finally put our father in the past."

After a moment's thought, Roslyn reasoned, "Well, if that's the case, I wouldn't worry about it, darling. After all, look what falling in love has done for us."

Groaning, he pulled her back down and into the tight circle of his arms. "Yeah, just look. You can't wipe the smile off my face."

"You know, I think you deserve a Halloween treat tonight," she murmured coyly. "And it has nothing to do with candy."

Chuckling, he rolled her onto her back. "I couldn't agree more."

* * * * *

Look for the next Men of the West book in September 2019 from Harlequin Special Edition!

And don't miss out on these other great stories by Stella Bagwell:

Guarding His Fortune
A Ranger for Christmas
The Little Maverick Matchmaker
Her Man on Three Rivers Ranch

Available now wherever Harlequin books and ebooks are sold.

Losing Miranda broke Matt Grimes's heart. And kept him from the knowledge of his pending fatherhood. Now Miranda Contreras has returned to Rocking Chair, Texas—with their eight-year-old daughter. Matt should be angry! What other secrets could Miranda be keeping? But all he sees is a chance to be the family they were meant to be.

Read on for a sneak preview of The Cowboy's Secret Family, *the next great book in* USA TODAY *bestselling author Judy Duarte's Rocking Chair Rodeo miniseries.*

When Matt looked up, she offered him a shy smile. "Like I said, I'm sorry. I should have told you that you were a father."

"You've got that right."

"I've made mistakes, but Emily isn't one of them. She's a great kid. So for now, let's focus on her."

"All right." Matt uncrossed his arms and raked a hand through his hair. "But just for the record, I would've done anything in my power to take care of you and Emily."

"I know." And that was why she'd walked away from him. Matt would have stood up to her father, challenged his threat, only to be knocked to his knees—and worse.

No, leaving town and cutting all ties with Matt was the only thing she could've done to protect him.

As she stood in the room where their daughter was conceived, as she studied the only man she'd ever loved, the memories crept up on her…the old feelings, too.

When she was sixteen, there'd been something about the fun-loving nineteen-year-old cowboy that had drawn her attention. And whatever it was continued to tug at her now. But she shook it off. Too many years had passed; too many tears had been shed.

Besides, an unwed single mother who was expecting another man's baby wouldn't stand a chance with a champion bull rider who had his choice of pretty cowgirls. And she'd best not forget that.

"Aw, hell," Matt said, as he ran a hand through his hair again and blew out a weary sigh. "Maybe you did Emily a favor by leaving when you did. Who knows what kind of father I would have made back then. Or even now."

HSEEXP0519